PROUD
of me

It's always been the two of us. Him and me.
Why has he started keeping secrets?

It's always been the two of us. Her and me.
Why doesn't she talk to me any more?

All I want is for my family to be...

PROUD

of me

SARAH HAGGER-HOLT

USBORNE

First published in the UK in 2021 by Usborne Publishing Ltd., Usborne House, 83-85 Saffron Hill, London EC1N 8RT, England. usborne.com

A CIP catalogue record for this book is available from the British Library.

ISBN 9781474966245 05348/1 JFMAMJJASON /20

Printed and bound in Great Britain by CPI Group (UK) Ltd, Croydon, CRO 4YY.

BECKY

When people ask about my family, I always say that Josh is my twin brother. It's easier that way. It saves a whole load of explaining.

But it's not exactly true.

We weren't even born on the same day. He's eight days younger than me – something I never let him forget. And he's not fully my brother, not in a blood-thicker-than-water, same-mother-same-father kind of way. But so what? Does that matter?

Isn't it enough that it's always been the two of us? In the baby photos: tiny heads peeping out from the matching fluffy blankets that Grandma knitted for us both. On our first day at school: standing stiff and awkward in our new uniforms, our eyes full of mischief

5

and Josh's hand squeezing mine. In our best clothes at our bar and bat mitzvahs – joint, of course. At every birthday party and family gathering, every holiday and holy day. Together.

The photos start even before we were born. My favourite is of two women, arms round each other as they pose for the camera, both with smiles as big as their bumps. One bump is Josh. The other is me. The women are our two mums: Ima – "Mum" in Hebrew – and Mum.

Ima usually takes the pictures, joking with us till we smile, and Mum prints them out and frames them. Unclip each one from its frame and you'll see her neat capitals written on the back – the date, the occasion, the cast of characters (left to right).

Josh asked her why once. "What's the point of all that labelling?" he said, just to wind her up. "You're not going to forget who we are, are you?"

Instead of answering, Mum sighed, crossed the room and pulled out a tatty cardboard box from the back of a cupboard. It was full of photos – some yellow-tinted colour Polaroids with thick white borders, but mostly ancient black-and-white shots of people with strange clothes and serious expressions.

We tipped up the box and spread the pictures out on the table, fingering the edges, turning them over to find faded, scrawly writing or nothing at all, picking them up to squint at what was going on in each image.

"Who are all these people?" I breathed.

"Precisely. Who *are* they?" said Mum. "We don't know. And that's why I label everything."

"But you must know something about them. I mean, you must have these photos for a reason," insisted Josh.

"Yes, okay." She smiled. "Of course there's a reason. These people are my family – your family too. I can't believe I haven't shown you them before."

She looked down at the mess of photos. "Great-grandparents, my mum's aunts and uncles, cousins, friends. Not one of them alive any more. No one now to explain who's who or to tell their stories or give away their secrets."

It felt sad when she said that, but there was something exciting about it too.

"It's like a mystery," I burst out. I was really into detective stories back then. "There are clues, if we can solve them. Like, if we knew when hats like this were in fashion" – I pointed at one picture of a group of women in elaborate bonnets, smiling in front of a fancy hotel –

"or when this hotel opened, we could work out what year these photos were taken, and *then* we could work out—"

Josh snorted.

I poked him. "What?"

"Well, we *could* do all of that, but it's just guessing, isn't it? We'd never know for sure if we were right."

That's totally Josh. Ima says that Josh will only believe something if he can touch it, taste it or see it. So like Mum. You can't fool either of them. Without Josh, I'd always be getting carried away with some ridiculous dream.

"Yeah, but that doesn't stop you wondering and wanting to know," I told him. "I bet there are things you want to know, even if it might seem pointless to try and find out."

Josh just shrugged and turned away. But I knew I was right. He might deny it to anyone else, even to Mum and Ima, but I knew there was one thing Josh had always wanted to find out.

"Hey, aren't you going to help put them away?" asked Mum, as we both started to wander off.

So we shuffled the photos into rough piles, shoving them back in the box, and, as we did, one caught my eye. A woman, a girl really, probably in her late teens, looking straight at the camera with a half-smile, like she'd just heard a really good joke and was trying not to laugh. She had a hat with flowers on and stiffly curled hair. The photo was old, faded, but her smile made her look totally alive. I flipped it over to see if there were any clues on the back about who she was.

"Look," I gasped, holding up the picture to Mum and pointing at the writing on the back. It was hard to read, but this was one word I'd recognize anywhere. My own name: Rebecca.

"Well, well," Mum said thoughtfully, sitting down and holding the picture up to the light. "That must be one of my grandma's sisters – they were a big family you know, nine children wasn't so unusual in those days. She *might* have mentioned a Rebecca. She'd be your great-great-aunt, I suppose."

"Was I named after her?" I asked eagerly.

"No, sorry."

She could see I looked disappointed, so she went on. "Ima and I chose your names together. We didn't name you after anyone. We wanted names that meant something. You know what Rebecca means, don't you?" I shook my head. "It means joining, like when two ropes are knotted together. Just like you, me, Ima and Josh are

9

all tied together as one family: two mums, two kids – and nothing can break us apart." She gently laced her fingers through mine so that our hands were linked together and smiled.

"What about me?" said Josh, hanging back, more interested now.

"Now, Joshua, that one was Ima's idea. It means 'salvation' or 'God is generous'. After all, we'd tried and tried for so long for one baby, and suddenly here were two on their way! Generous indeed…"

She shut the box with a snap. Conversation over. "You can keep that picture if you like, Becky."

I held onto that photograph. After that, I decided that I didn't want to be a detective any more. I wanted to be a photographer – to take pictures that could make a person or place come alive to whoever saw them, just like great-great-aunt Rebecca had come alive to me. I wanted nothing more or less than to make magic.

Three years later, that picture is still tucked in the back of my diary. It usually remains hidden between the pages, but sometimes I get it out, and I look at great-great-aunt Rebecca and wonder what secrets she's keeping behind that smile.

JOSH

Things that annoy me:

1. People saying "Yeah, but which one's your *real* mum?" (They both are, stupid.)

2. Hair in the shower. (It drives me nuts. It's gross. Everyone in the house has long hair except me. Mum's is straight and fair but going slightly grey. Ima's hair is dark and curly, and so is Becky's. I find clumps of it in the plughole, strands stuck to the shower curtain. It gets everywhere. Ima told me I must be the only teenage boy in the world who cleans the shower without being asked. I said, "I wouldn't have to if you didn't leave it so disgusting and hairy." She said, "Don't let me stop you.")

3. Having to learn stuff off by heart for tests. (What's the point? You can google it all anyway.)
4. People who talk like they are using exclamation marks all the time. (Archie, Becky's best friend, does this. Not everything can be that exciting all the time, can it? Just chill.)
5. Not knowing who my dad is.

It took me a while to realize that having a dad was a thing. Of course, I knew that most of my friends had dads, and I knew that I didn't. I like to think I was quite an observant kid. But not *all* of them had dads and, anyway, you didn't often see dads around. Not like people's mums, who were always at our house or hanging about chatting while we played on the swings down the park.

True, families in books usually had dads, but then all sorts of things happened in books, like talking animals or trips to space, so that didn't necessarily mean anything in the real world.

Once I was at school, I realized that although some people's dads weren't around much, or at all, everyone seemed to have one, somewhere. And they all assumed that I did too.

I think I was about six when I first asked Ima straight out why I didn't have a dad. We were in the car on the way back from swimming, Becky and I warm and dry and in our onesies, ready to head straight to bed when we got home.

"A dad?" echoed Ima. "You know why you don't have a dad, Josh. It's because you've got two mums. Think how lucky you are. Not many people can say they've got two mums. That's something special, isn't it? Two mums." She paused. "And you've got Grandpa and Uncle Noah too."

"Yeah, I s'pose."

But that wasn't what I'd meant. Having a dad wasn't anything to do with how many mums you had, was it? Couldn't you have two mums *and* a dad? We didn't even see Uncle Noah or Grandpa very often. I loved them, but neither of them were my dad. Loads of people have uncles and grandpas and *still* have a dad.

"What about the kind man?" I asked after a minute of hard thinking.

"What kind man?" asked Ima.

"You know," Becky piped up helpfully. "The kind man who gave you the sperm so you could have us."

"Oh," said Ima. "The donor…"

She and Mum always explained everything to us using

the correct words, even from when we were really small. Mum's a nurse, so she's not squeamish about talking about bodies and that kind of stuff, and Ima's never embarrassed about anything.

"Sweetheart, that's different. That's not like having a dad. He was just someone who helped us out, that's all. We didn't even meet him. We were lucky that we could get help from the doctors and from the donor to have you both, so that Becky could grow in my tummy and you could grow in Mum's. And we love you both very, very much."

"But *could* we meet him?" I asked. "One day, I mean, not today. Cos he's sort of like our dad, isn't he?"

"Well," said Ima slowly, "when you are eighteen, if you still want to meet the donor, then you can try and find out about him and see if he wants to meet you."

"Eighteen!" I gasped, outraged. "That's years and years and years away."

Ima didn't reply. It was still light outside and my head was full of questions, but the car was warm and my body tired out from swimming.

Becky and I had lessons together, us and about twelve other kids. I was always the slowest. Not like Becky. She could have swum fast and far enough to be in the higher class with the bigger kids. She never said anything, but I

14

knew she went slowly so that we could stay in the same class together. Swimming always wore me out. I was starting to drift off when Becky broke the silence.

"I made a card for Grandpa today at school."

"Did you?" said Ima. "That's nice. It isn't his birthday though, not till November."

"Not for his birthday, for *Father's* Day," Becky explained. "Everyone was making cards for their dads, so Mrs Williams asked whether we'd like to make cards for our grandpa and I said yes."

"Oh, I see," said Ima thoughtfully. "What about you, Josh, did you make a card for Grandpa too?"

"No!" I shouted. She didn't understand anything. "Grandpa's not my dad. Grandpa's *Mum's* dad. *She* should make him a card for Father's Day, not me. Father's Day is for fathers, that's why it's called Father's Day, and I haven't got one."

"Oh, Joshy," was all Ima said, as she slowed down and parked outside our house.

And even though that was years ago and we don't really talk about it now, I still wonder what it will be like to meet our donor one day. And just in my head, without saying anything to anyone else, I've started to think about him as, not just our donor, but our dad.

BECKY

It's the start of term, our last term in Year Eight. It's a perfect spring day and this morning everything feels brand-new. Like that song we used to sing in assembly at primary school, you know, "Morning Has Broken", that one.

I still don't know what "broken" means. Surely broken is a bad thing, like ruined or spoiled? Yet in the song it's good, like something bursting into life. What's that all about? Ima would just shrug if I asked her. She says I overthink things, that I should take life as it comes and the details will take care of themselves. She's kind of right, but kind of wrong too. After all, how will I ever become a really great photographer unless I learn to look closely at everything? That's *all* about paying attention to the details.

I suppose most people will have to drag themselves out of bed today, groaning that it's the start of a new term. Josh was stumbling around like a zombie this morning. He's not been up before ten all holiday. But I've always been okay with getting up early.

This is my favourite term: spring melts into summer; school gets quieter as the Year Elevens and Thirteens gradually disappear into study leave and exams; the evenings get longer and the mornings brighter and there's a great light for taking photos.

But today feels like even more than just a warm April morning. Today feels…charged, electric.

"Beckster!" It's Archie. He sashays his way through the crowds of students, swinging his bag behind him. He drapes his arm around me, and we walk together through the doors into school. "How *are* you, hun?"

"Really good," I say, beaming. "This morning's beautiful."

"Take it easy, babes, you'll be bursting into song next!" He pulls back, holding me at arm's length, and looks into my eyes. "So, how much did you miss me?"

"Tons. Seeing you's the best thing about being back at school." I grin. "How was your dad's?"

Archie grimaces. Every holiday, since his parents

split up, Archie and his little brother go and stay with their dad in his new home, in a tiny village in Somerset. Archie hates it. "Eurgh, you know, all scarecrows and cowpats and country bumpkins."

"It was not!" I exclaim.

"What do you know?"

"I have *been* out of Watford, you know. Anyway, your dad's not a country bumpkin."

"Not far off. He's always in his wellies and now he wears the most tasteless mac ever!" Archie rolls out the "r" at the end of the last word. "Although I'm not sure if a mac could ever be taste*ful*, to be honest. Every day he dragged us out for 'just a little stroll'. Oh my god, miles and miles of rain and mud. 'This'll make men out of you', he kept saying. As if."

"Well, you're back where you belong now," I say, pushing open the door to the 8R classroom.

"Too true. Do you want to know the first thing I did when I got back to civilization?"

"Charge up your phone?"

"*Charging* my phone wasn't the problem, babes. My dad does at *least* have electricity – small mercies – but no reception. You had to virtually hang out of the window to get even the tiniest bit of signal. Nightmare. Anyway, no, the *first* thing I put on was one of those facial masks. Bliss. All that dirt and mud out of my pores at last. Feel my skin – feel it!"

I reach up and stroke his cheek. "Beautiful," I say. "Soft as—"

"Anyway," Archie interrupts, perching on one of the desks in the back row. "I've been going on and on about me. How are you? How is that gorgeous brother of yours?"

"Yeah, Josh is all right." I pause. Is that really true? I realize that I didn't see that much of Josh this holiday. He was mostly up in his room or out playing football or on his bike. And when he *was* around, well, he was quiet, distant, distracted.

Anyone who knows how much time Archie and I spend together thinks he must be my boyfriend. Anyone who hasn't actually *met* Archie, that is. Anyone who's spent five minutes with Archie knows that's never going to happen.

It doesn't bother me. I don't fancy Archie. I never have. We've been friends since forever though, leading everyone else in primary school in playground make-believe games, whispering and giggling our way through every class.

When Archie came out at the start of Year Eight, I was the first to know.

My first loyalty is to Josh, it's always been him and me, but Archie comes a very close second. Josh keeps my feet on the ground, but Archie sends my imagination spinning.

Josh is home, Archie is away.

I know, I'm lucky.

"Anyway, I've got some exciting news."

"Oh yes?"

"Well, I bumped into Alex this morning…"

I roll my eyes and pretend to yawn. "I *thought* you said exciting."

Alex is this boy in Year Eleven who Archie's obsessed with. Archie's always making me hang back in the corridors with him, so he can "accidentally" run into Alex. He is also one of the very few other out gay kids in the school, which Archie thinks is amazing.

"No, stop it, don't sigh like that, it doesn't suit you. Anyway, I bumped into Alex—"

"You said that already."

"Just listen, why don't you? Stop interrupting." He assumes his stern look – which never fails to make me burst out laughing. "Ready now?"

"Okay, okay, go on then, impress me."

"You know the Pride group idea, right?" He waits

20

until I nod in agreement, before carrying on. "So, Alex spoke to Ms Bryant about it before Easter, about whether we'd be allowed to set one up here…"

"Why Ms Bryant?" I interrupt. "What's it got to do with her?" Ms Bryant teaches us science as well as being head of Year Eight.

Archie shrugs. "I don't know. He just said something about how she offered to help. Anyway, that's not the point. Alex explained to her how it would be a group for LGBTQ students and straight ones, whoever wants to support it really. She went away and read lots of stuff about it over the holidays and talked to the rest of the staff. And Alex told me this morning that she said yes."

Archie's always been a bit extra, a bit over the top, someone who attracts attention. I don't know if it's because he's gay or because that's just the way he is. Whatever it is, he makes the world a more exciting place to be in. And I love it. But not everyone does. He acts like he's not bothered by the nasty comments or sly looks he sometimes gets, but he must be, a bit. I would be. I know this group will be somewhere safe, where he doesn't need to pretend anything, where he can relax and be himself. Not just for him, for anyone who needs it. That's why it matters so much.

"Really? Archie, that's brilliant." I am so happy for him.

"I know." He grins like a little kid who's been given an ice cream. "Apparently, Ms B thinks it would be good for our personal and social development or something. And that Ofsted'll like it. And something about St John's having one already. I think I'm the first to know, after Alex. And now you, of course."

"So what happens next?"

"I don't know, I guess we set up our first meeting. You will be coming, won't you? I mean, anyone can come, you don't have to be gay. And it won't clash with photography club, I'll make sure of it." He suddenly looks anxious.

"Course I'm coming. Got to be there for my bestie." I give his arm a squeeze. "Anyway, can you imagine what Mum and Ima would say if I didn't support it?"

Actually, I'm not sure what Mum and Ima *would* say. They were super supportive when Archie came out, but when it comes to what they want for our own family? I don't know. Mostly I think all they want is for us to blend in, not draw attention to ourselves – to play it safe.

Would they want me to join the group or not? Would it be too "out there" for them? Would they think me joining is all about them – even if it's not?

22

"Look," Archie whispers suddenly, breaking into my thoughts. "Two o'clock. Who is that?" I turn to my right. Jon and Nazim are a couple of rows ahead of us, leaning back with their feet on their desks, arguing about football like they always do.

"Not that way. I meant ten o'clock. New girl." I peer over to the other side of the classroom. He grabs my arm. "No, don't look like you're looking."

"What? You told me to!" I carry on staring. "Anyway, she can't see, she's got her back to us."

There's a girl in the second row who I've never seen before. I can't see much of her now – just the back of her head. She's got blonde hair, short at the back, so her neck's just visible above the collar of her school shirt. She already stands out – most girls here wear their hair long. A small silver hoop glints at the top of her ear. She moves, as if to look round, and I feel the breath catch in my throat.

I look away and find I can breathe normally again. "Funny time of year to start a new school," I say to Archie.

He leans in, voice low. "Do you think she's been expelled from somewhere else?"

I shrug. "Maybe her parents have split up…"

"Or gone to prison…"

"Or died in a tragic accident…"

"Or just returned from a top-secret diplomatic mission…"

"…And that's why she's had to come here in the middle of the year."

Before we can dream up any more wild theories, Mr Ross comes in, claps his hands and starts talking.

The murmurs die down. Nazim and Jon swiftly take their feet off the desks, and everyone else hurries to find their seats. I keep snatching glances at the new girl – who is she?

I like Mr Ross. As teachers go, he's pretty good. He's nice, but not a pushover, and he really does listen when you tell him things. Some teachers barely make an effort to learn your name, but with Mr Ross, you feel that he actually likes each one of us, and that makes everyone like him.

He rattles through registration, and then turns to the new girl at the front. "Everyone, this is Carli," he says. "Carli's joining us this term, the newest member of 8R. I'm sure you'll make her very welcome."

He casts his eyes around the classroom. "Now… Serena, would you be able to keep an eye out for Carli, show her around, make sure she knows what's going on, that kind of thing?" Serena – studious, reliable and a little bit dull – always gets picked for jobs like this. Normally, I wouldn't be bothered. Today, I wish it was me.

The rest of the day rushes by. Josh and I are in different forms – an effort by the school to make sure we "mix" – so as usual I don't see him much except at breaks or lunchtime. Before long everything about school feels totally normal again. It seems impossible that only yesterday we were still on holiday. Like when it's the middle of winter and you can't remember what summer's like or imagine ever feeling warm again. And through everything – handing in homework, catching up on everyone's news, queuing in the canteen, dashing from class to class – there is the new girl, shadowed by Serena. On the edge of my vision. Just out of earshot. At the back of my mind. Carli.

The final lesson of the day is science. It's over in the labs – an old block tucked away behind the sports hall. They keep talking about refurbishing the building, but nothing happens. So it's been left to quietly crumble away.

Archie and I start to make our way over, and I'm still rummaging in my bag as I walk along.

"Argh, I haven't got my book. I thought it was in here somewhere, but…"

"Oh, Becks, are you sure? What if it's crushed underneath something else in that enormous sack of yours?"

"No, it's really not." I shove all the loose papers that I've dislodged back into my bag. "I'll just dash back to my locker. I'll only be a second – less, a nanosecond. Wait for me – no, actually, don't wait, go and grab us a seat at the back. I'll see you over there."

Ms Bryant won't be happy even if I'm only a couple of minutes late, especially as it's the first day of term. I run back, nipping quickly through the corridors, slowing down only when I pass a classroom door. I flick open my locker and grab the book from the top. I spin round – and Carli is standing quietly right behind me.

I'm so surprised to see someone there that I drop the book. It feels like I've magically made her appear just by thinking about her.

"What the…" I stutter. "I mean, what are you…?"

"Sorry," she says, picking up the book from the floor and handing it back to me. In my confusion, I shove the book quickly back in my locker and slam the door shut.

"I didn't mean to startle you. I'm Carli. I saw you in homeroom earlier. It's just, I'm looking for the science lab. They gave me this map here," she continues, holding out a piece of paper covered in different coloured splodges connected by dotted lines, "but it makes no sense."

"It's okay, I've got science too. You'd better follow me – that map looks next to useless. What happened to Serena?"

"Ah, she had a violin lesson or something." She shrugs. "Whatever, I lost her."

"Hey…" I've suddenly realized what's different about Carli. "You're American."

"Ten out of ten," she says wearily. "And before you ask – no, I haven't met the president and I don't know any Hollywood stars. Okay?"

"Who's asking anything?"

"Sorry, it's just been a long day, y'know." She smiles. I would have sworn no one could have teeth that white. "The moment anyone hears my accent they ask me the same old questions. It's like no one's ever met a real live American before, just seen them on TV."

"Not everyone's like that," I say, biting back my own stream of questions.

"I guess people back home would be just the same." She deliberately makes her accent sound stronger. "'Have y'all met the royal family?' and 'What cute little cars you have – are those really for driving?'"

27

I burst out laughing. "Actually, I *have* met the queen," I reply.

"No way!"

"Well, not *met* exactly. But I have seen her. From a distance."

Carli raises her eyebrows. "Go on…"

"She opened a new wing at the hospital where my mum works, like ten years ago. We all went along to watch. I was in the crowd, up on…" I hesitate, never sure when to explain to new people that I've got two mums. "…On my mum's shoulders."

"Wow, wait till I tell my friends back home about that – I reckon if I say I'm your friend, then I'm practically on the guest list for Buckingham Palace. Right?"

"Right," I say, smiling.

"But I don't even know your name yet."

"Oh, sorry, it's Becky."

"Well, Becky, can you show me where the science labs are? I don't want to get into trouble, not on my first day anyway."

I've been so focused on Carli that I'd totally forgotten the time.

"Oh no, we're so going to have to run."

I grab my bag. One good thing about being this late is

that at least there's no one else in the corridors to get in our way.

"Don't worry," Carli says in my ear just as we approach the closed lab door. "I'll take the blame for this one."

There's no way we can sneak in unnoticed. The benches all face the door, which is heavy and old and creaks loudly however gently you try to open it. Archie looks at me and opens his hands in a *Where have you been?* gesture. But before Ms Bryant has a chance to say anything, Carli starts explaining.

"I'm really sorry we're so late. Today's my first day. I got kinda lost, Becky was helping me out." She smiles her winning smile. Serena, in the front row with an empty seat next to her, looks sheepish.

"Well, take a seat quickly now, both of you. Welcome to Larkhall, Carli, I'm sure you'll get the hang of things soon. Now, everyone, there's nothing to talk about, back to page seventy-one."

I slide into my seat next to Archie and reach in my bag for my book. Not there. Archie sees me rummaging, sighs, and moves his book so it's resting between us.

JOSH

I shuffle into the kitchen, shake the last two slices of bread out of the bag and shove them in the toaster. Breakfast? Lunch? The clock says just after midday, so it could be either.

It's the first Saturday after the start of term, so I deserve a lie-in. There's a scribbled note from Ima on the side, saying when she'll be back from shul – synagogue – with a reminder to put the dishwasher on and a little smiley face at the bottom.

In the weeks before our bar and bat mitzvah – the ceremony that's supposed to mark the start of our adult lives – we *had* to go to shul every Saturday morning. But that was back last autumn. Since then I've not always been so great at getting out of bed in time. Ima doesn't nag us about it, because she says she doesn't want to turn into *her* mother, but if we miss more than a week, she does start making comments. Not that we know *what* Ima's mum is like. Or her dad. He died a long time ago and Ima argued with her mum, ages before we were born. We've never met our grandparents on her side. Ima says that we are all the family she needs.

If I'm honest, it's not just the early start that puts me off. I *can* get up when I really need to, however much Becky teases me about being lazy. It's weird, I thought marking my bar mitzvah was mostly about making Ima and Mum happy. Oh, and the cake and the presents. But, I don't know, standing up there in front of everyone, reading the Hebrew and knowing that people have done this for hundreds, maybe even thousands of years, passing the traditions from one generation to another…well, it freaked me out a bit.

It's that bit in the service where the scroll is handed from parent to child. When Mum and Ima stepped up to the front, smiling proudly, to pass the heavy scroll to Becky and me for our readings, it felt different from every other bar mitzvah I've been to. Our friends and family were there – Uncle Noah with Mum and Ima in the front row, next to Grandma and Grandpa even though they never normally come to synagogue. Ima's parents weren't there, but that's nothing unusual, they retired back to Israel when we were little so we barely see them now. Yet something, some*one*, was missing. I've always felt it, that gap, but this was different. It suddenly felt screamingly, blindingly obvious who was missing: my dad. The ceremony is supposed to be all about becoming an adult – but how can I ever hope to do that without first knowing who I really am?

"Morning!" shouts Becky cheerily from the living room, interrupting my thoughts. There's a pause. "Or is it afternoon?" she continues.

"Shut up," I reply. "It's the weekend, in case you hadn't noticed. There's no need to be up at the crack of dawn every Saturday, is there?"

Becky was up before me, but not early enough to go to shul either. She's still in her pyjamas, sprawled on the sofa and eating a bowl of cereal.

"Anyway," I grumble, "you can talk."

She grins at me, then pretends to look surprised. "Oh yes, so I can! Thanks for pointing it out."

Becky enjoys teasing me in the mornings. When we were little and shared a room – our beds each against opposite walls – she used to pull the covers off me in the mornings or tickle my feet to wake me up. I'd get my own back though, making spooky noises after Mum or Ima turned out our light, just when she was trying to get to sleep.

It sounds mean, but it wasn't, not really. It's just that, because we know each other so well, we also know exactly how to wind each other up. And when to stop. Sometimes it feels like Becky knows what I'm thinking before I even know myself. No one else knows me like that – not even Ima, not even Mum.

Right now, she's got the TV on while she reads a magazine and scrolls through messages on her phone. Her maths book is on the sofa, a ruler marking her place, and pens are scattered everywhere. Her empty cereal bowl is balanced on the arm of the sofa. I move her junk out of the way and flop down beside her.

"Started homework already?" I ask, balancing my plate on her maths book like it's a tray.

She shrugs. "Yeah, well, might as well get it done. There's not much. Archie's coming round later and—"

"Really? Archie? Come on…it's *supposed* to be a day of rest."

"I wouldn't worry," she fires back, "it looks like you've rested enough for one day already."

33

I eat my toast while Becky plays with her spoon – first using it to scrape non-existent crumbs out of her empty bowl, and then twirling it between her fingers. She always fiddles with something when she's thinking about what to say.

"Josh, have you spoken to the new girl yet? What do you think of her?" she says, all casual.

"What, the one with blonde hair? In your form?"

She nods. "How many new girls are there in Year Eight?"

"Haven't really seen much of her. I haven't had any classes with her yet. Jayden Andrews thinks she's hot though. He's been going on and on about how he's going to ask her out. How her lucky day is coming soon."

"Really?"

"Well, you know what he's like. He's just saying it. Don't think he's even spoken to her yet."

"Jayden? Really?"

She sounds upset.

"What's the big deal, Becks?" I look up at her. I can always tell when Becky's hiding something from me. "Hey, it's not that *you* fancy Jayden, is it?"

"Jayden? Eurgh, no." She screws up her face in disgust, like when Mum "forgets" that Becky hates mushrooms and hides them in the pasta sauce.

34

"Cos I can put in a word for you if you like…"

"I'm not interested in Jayden," she snaps. "Or *any* of your friends. I don't even know why you hang out with him."

"Chill. I'm just trying to help. Anyway, what about the new girl?" I ask. "What's she like?"

Becky flicks over another page in her magazine. "Hmm…what?" she says vaguely.

"The new girl." I sigh. "Carli – what's she like?"

"Oh, nice enough, I guess. Did you know she's American?"

"That's cool. So what's she doing here?"

Becky shrugs, like she's lost interest in the conversation. The conversation which she started.

Whatever. I can't be bothered with Becky's moods right now. I've got other things to worry about.

Mum's at work and Ima will be at shul for ages, catching up on everyone's news. Just enough time for my investigations.

I've been working out the best places to look. I know all the usual places they keep stuff, but there's a few I can rule out straight away.

It's not going to be stuck on the fridge, where Mum and Ima keep things like money-off vouchers or letters from school or bills to pay – that's too public. Or at the bottom of Ima's wardrobe, even though that's the classic place to hide birthday presents.

Looking in the attic is a last resort. It would be a good place to hide something, but terrible if you wanted to try and find it again. I haven't been up there for ages, but I know it's full of stuff, jam-packed with boxes and bags. It would take ages if I had to search through all of those.

That leaves the filing cabinet in the box room. It's grey and squat with only two drawers and a ridiculous tasselled cloth draped over the top to try and make it look nice. It still looks ugly. Mum got it at an office closing-down sale, along with one of those chairs on wheels that Becky and I used to dare each other to spin round and round on until we felt sick. The cabinet's locked, but I know where the key is – attached to a bit of string taped to the back. Hardly top security.

I'll start with the filing cabinet, it's the most obvious place.

I squeeze my plate into the dishwasher, switch it on and head upstairs. I close the door to the box room quietly behind me. My heart is beating fast. I feel like a burglar in my own house.

The filing cabinet drawer squeaks a little when I open

it. It sounds loud, but Becky won't hear it over the noise of the TV and the dishwasher. I tell myself it's okay, I'm not doing anything wrong. Mum and Ima have never specifically said not to look in here. I guess they assumed we wouldn't want to.

Inside, the cabinet is so organized. This must be Mum. Folders arranged alphabetically with all the documents and papers tucked in neatly.

I start with "B" for "birth". And the system works – there are our birth certificates, with their official red writing and old-fashioned fonts. Mum's name on mine. Ima's on Becky's. It feels weird that Ima's name is not anywhere on mine, just like Mum's isn't on Becky's, even though it's obvious that Becky and I are brother and sister and that Mum and Ima are both our parents.

Even more weird is the empty space on both birth certificates in the box marked "Father". I can't stop staring at the blank. It bothers me. I just want to know who he is, that's all. A name, a face. To know who he is, and to know who I am.

The birth certificates are no help. Next I try "C" for "clinic", "F" for "fertility", even "S" for "sperm donor". Nothing. I slam the drawer shut in frustration. This was a stupid idea. Of course there won't be anything here.

I pause and listen – still quiet downstairs, apart from the churning of the dishwasher and the sound of the TV. I take a deep breath to calm myself. One last try.

I flick through the files as methodically as I can, telling myself not to be too disappointed as, one after another, they give nothing away. I reach the final file, "XYZ", but when I try and reach right to the back of the drawer, something gets in the way. I put my hand in and dislodge a crumpled piece of paper. I smooth it out against the top of the cabinet. It's the printout of an email. Not just any email, but an invoice. The date at the top is from before Becky and I were born, and at the bottom is the name of a fertility clinic.

And I know. I've found what I'm looking for.

The front door slams.

"I'm home! And guess what I've got to show you."

Ima's voice floats up the stairs. I take a quick picture of the invoice on my phone then shove it back where I found it, slide the drawer shut, turn the key and smooth out the cloth on the top of the cabinet.

I head back downstairs. On the outside, nothing's changed. But inside, my heart is racing. So close.

I'm kind of glad that Ima's come back early. I need time to think about what to do next. Time to talk to Becky.

But I don't know if I can. Not about this.

Ima lays out some sheets of paper on the coffee table, and Becky and I huddle round to get a closer look.

"I talked to Neil today," she says. "About the cake. He's going to do it, it's all booked in and he's promised not to say a word to Mum."

Neil and his wife Sandy go to the same synagogue as us. They're two of Mum and Ima's oldest friends and are always round our house. They have three daughters – all younger than Becky and me. Neil runs a catering company and does weddings, funerals, everything. He makes the most amazing cakes I've ever eaten. He talks a lot, but he's nice too – he pretends not to see when I sneak a pinch of crumbs from the side of the plate or even help myself to an extra slice. He always jokes that he and I should look out for each other because we're both men outnumbered in houses full of women.

"That's brilliant about the cake," says Becky. "One more thing off the list and still weeks to go."

"The most *important* thing – you can't have a proper birthday party without a cake!" agrees Ima. "Look at these." She points at the page of sketches, showing the different layers of chocolate cake with salted caramel icing – Mum's favourite – and sugar flowers on the top.

"Wow, it's like something from *Bake Off*!" sighs Becky.

I nod. It *is* impressive, but I'm still worried.

"Josh, you're quiet. What do you think?" says Ima gently.

"It looks great," I say, after a pause. "Really great. It's just, well, do you think Mum would really want a surprise party? I mean, she doesn't usually like a lot of fuss."

"Oh, Josh," groans Becky. "Don't be so boring!"

"No, Becks, Josh is right. She *doesn't* normally have a lot of fuss on her birthday. It's always pretty low-key, right? She'd never think of organizing a party for herself." I nod. Ima is starting to get it. "But that's *exactly* why a surprise party is such a good idea – she's waited so long for a proper celebration. She deserves it, doesn't she? Anyway, you don't get to be fifty every day of the week."

"I s'pose."

Becky and Ima are so excited about this party. There's no talking them out of it. Maybe they're right – perhaps this is what Mum has always been hoping for.

"Do you really think she doesn't suspect anything?" asks Becky.

"Not a thing!" says Ima gleefully. "Everyone's been sworn to secrecy. And I'm getting loads more replies to my messages every day. People she hasn't seen for decades. I even tracked down a couple of her friends from school. Imagine. Even people who can't come are sending pictures and messages."

If everyone that Ima's got in touch with comes, the house will be packed. It's pretty impressive. I mean, she's rubbish with social media normally, yet she's still managed to find loads of Mum's friends from years ago. Even the ones who've changed their names or look completely different now.

A thought sparks in my mind. An exciting thought. Even if I can't trace my dad through the fertility clinic, there *will* be other ways to find him. Everyone's on social media somewhere, if you look long enough and hard enough. No one can totally disappear.

Becky nudges me. "What are you dreaming about, Josh?"

"Oh, nothing. Just don't *ever* organize a surprise party for me," I whisper to her. "Not even when I'm fifty." I can't think of anything worse – the stress of having to be nice to everyone all at once, being the centre of everyone's attention. And not even knowing beforehand. No warning, no time to prepare.

"It's okay," she whispers back. "I wouldn't dare. It would be wasted on you anyway. I know you don't like surprises. I'd quite like one though, you know, one day – just saying…"

"Okay. One day. Let's get Mum's out of the way first though."

"Out of the way?" says Becky, incredulous. "It's a *party*, Josh, not a test. It's not about 'getting it out of the way', it's about enjoying it."

"Yeah, I s'pose."

"Anyway, you'd *never* be able to keep a surprise party secret from me. I can see right through you. No secrets between us, little bro." She smiles, and I go cold. Does she already know? Should I just tell her now instead of keeping it bottled up?

There's a moment…but then she turns away, singing to herself, and goes to the kitchen to help Ima get lunch ready.

BECKY

In school on Monday, I look out for Carli. We've still only spoken once. All I know about her is that she's American. That's it.

But it's Archie, not me, who spots her first. She's sitting in the canteen at a table by herself, eating a salad, looking still and composed despite the bustle and noise all around her.

"Hey," says Archie, nudging me. "Look, it's the new girl. Let's go take her under our wing!"

"Her name's Carli," I object, "not 'the new girl'." I've been hoping to bump into Carli all morning, yet now that she's right in front of me, I feel too shy to go over. I pull Archie back. "Perhaps we shouldn't disturb her. She might not want to talk to us. She might be waiting

for someone or…I don't know…thinking about things."
I tail off weakly.

"Oh come *on*! Of course she wants to talk to us.
Anyway, after last week, you two are practically best
mates already!"

"But what about the others? They're saving us a space."
I gesture over to a table of girls from our form at the far
end of the canteen. But Archie's already gone. He marches
over to Carli and slaps his tray down on the table
beside her.

"Hey, I'm Archie," he announces and sits down. I
hang back nervously. It's weird how much I want them
to like each other when I've barely spoken to Carli myself.

"Hey, Archie." Carli smiles back. Her smile is like
someone turning on a light. "We have math together,
don't we?" Then, before Archie can answer, she spots me
trailing behind him. "Hi, Becky – thanks for getting
me to science last week. Don't worry, I've been studying
the map and I think I'm kinda getting the hang of
things now."

"Well, you found your way to the canteen," I say.

"This is the canteen?" Carli says, eyes wide. "Oh no,
I thought this was the sports hall." She makes a show of
looking around in mock horror. "Hmm, come to think

44

of it, maybe you're right. This map really does suck."

"Are you into sport then?" asks Archie, smiling. I can tell he likes her already. I feel strangely proud, like I discovered her.

"Yeah, anything that involves running, jumping, hitting a ball – I'm right there," says Carli.

Archie does a little shudder.

"Not your thing then?" Carli asks him.

He shakes his head.

"Not even basketball? But you're so tall!"

"Yeah, but you haven't seen how uncoordinated I am. I'd be a danger to everyone else on the team!"

"So what do you play?" I ask, keen to get the conversation back to Carli.

"Well, pretty much anything – softball's my favourite though." She looks at our blank faces. "You know – oh, maybe you don't."

"What's softball?" I ask.

"Kind of like baseball. You know baseball, right?"

"But with a soft ball?" hazards Archie. "That sounds like my kind of sport. Less risk of getting your teeth knocked out by something fast and hard."

"Actually, no, sorry. The ball's just as hard as in baseball – but bigger."

"Bigger? That's even worse!" says Archie. "Although I guess that means there's slightly more chance I'd be able to hit it – if I couldn't duck in time."

Carli grins. "Anyway, I guess I won't be playing softball here, if English people haven't even heard of it. Unless I start my own team. What about you guys, what are you into? Not sports, I guess."

"No, but my brother is," I say. "He's on the football team. But, well, photography's more my thing."

"Wow, cool."

"Yeah, Becky's really good," gushes Archie. "She even set up a photography club after school. Now the art department's going to offer GCSE photography because so many people have got into it. And her photos are amazing! She's like a real professional."

"Archie!" I murmur, warning him to shut up. I'm blushing. I love talking about photography, but I don't want Carli to think that I'm boasting about my skills before she's even seen a single one of my pictures.

"That's so cool. What kind of pictures do you take? Like, is it people or landscapes or, I don't know, like those really close-up arty shots where you can't see what it is but it looks beautiful?"

I laugh. "A bit of everything really. I like taking shots

of people best, photos that tell a story. I'd love to be a photojournalist one day, you know, reporting from war zones or really remote places that hardly anyone's been to before. But so far I haven't been much further than my cousin's wedding in north London!"

"I'd love to see some of your photos." She looks straight at me and I know she means it. She's not just being polite or so desperate to make friends in a new school that she'll hang out with anyone who's nice to her. Her eyes are bright blue and they sparkle.

"Maybe you could come round to my house after school one time and see them?" I blurt out. "That is, only if you want to. Maybe not Thursday, that's photography club, but any other night. Although, I mean, Thursday's probably okay too if you want…"

I'm just burbling on now. Archie looks at me in surprise. He knows I'd never normally suggest missing photography club, but Carli beams at me. That smile again.

"I'd love to. I'll need to check with my mom first. She's not that happy about me doing stuff on school nights, not while we're still settling in and all. But what about Friday?"

"Yeah, okay, Friday, great."

"Ahem." Archie pretend-coughs. "I'm here too. What about me? Aren't I invited?"

I had sort of forgotten about Archie, just for a moment.

"What *about* you? Mum says you practically live at our house anyway. Of course you can come round."

"Oh, I thought you'd never ask! Actually, I can't do Friday. Soz. Mum's working late and I need to be home to look after The Little Horror." "The Little Horror" is what Archie calls his younger brother, Mark. Mark isn't horrible at all really, but he *is* little. He's nine, nearly ten, and next to Archie he looks tiny. Maybe he'll have a growth spurt soon, like Archie did in Year Seven, and Archie will have to think up a new nickname for him.

Archie's always fun to be around, but I'm secretly looking forward to it being just Carli and me on Friday. Well, just Carli and me and Mum and Ima and Josh.

"So when will you tell her?" asks Archie, as we stack our trays and leave the canteen.

"Tell her what?"

"You know," he whispers loudly, "about the having-two-mums thing?"

"Oh, that."

"Yes, that."

Back in primary school, I didn't have to tell anyone

48

about my mums. At the start of each year, if there was a new teacher, Mum and Ima would come into school and explain to them about our family. And that was it. There weren't any problems – or if there were, no one told me or Josh about them. Mum and Ima would take turns dropping us off or picking us up, and both come to parents' evenings and school concerts when they didn't have to work. Everyone knew them. They were just… around.

But there was one time I remember in Year Four. A big game of football at lunchtime. It began with just our class, then Year Five and even some Year Sixes started joining in too. Mostly boys, but a handful of girls as well. Each team was huge and the game gradually took over the whole playground. No one planned it, it just happened. Anyone who wasn't playing was watching – Mrs Williams, our teacher, too. The whistle was hanging loose round her neck, and she looked like she'd forgotten it was up to her to blow it and send us back into our classrooms for the afternoon.

It seemed like Kyle in our class would score the final goal. The decider. It was such an easy kick. Kyle was right there, ready. Yet, at the last minute, something went wrong. He slipped, and the ball rolled away to the side.

The other team went mad – cheering, slapping each other on the back, before running off to collect their jumpers from the pile by the fencing.

Kyle was left by himself, bright red, trying not to cry. Some of the bigger Year Six boys clustered round him.

"Why did you do such a gay shot?" one shouted at him.

"Yeah, stupid gay boy," said another.

And suddenly Mrs Williams was right next to them. I'd never seen her move so fast. She was almost as red in the face as Kyle.

"You do not use the word 'gay' as a term of abuse at this school! Or anywhere," she shouted. "Understand?"

The boys shuffled. "But, Miss – didn't you see? We could have won the game if it wasn't for him."

"*But* nothing – inside now or you'll be going straight to Mr Phelps."

She turned her back to the boys and shooed away the small crowd which had gathered to watch. But she beckoned to Josh and me.

"Becky, Josh – are you all right?" she asked gently with a hand on each of our shoulders. We nodded, unsure what had happened, unsure why we might not be all right. No one had shouted at *us*. We were still out of breath from the game. We knew the word "gay" was something to do with Mum and Ima, but it wasn't a bad thing or a name you called someone. Not until that day.

At Larkhall it's different. I've got so used to people saying "gay" like it's just another word for "stupid" that I hardly notice it any more. I take a while now to tell new people about my family. I wait till I've really got to know them and know that they'll be okay. But with Carli, for some reason, I'm not worried.

"She's nice," I protest to Archie. "She'll be cool with it. It's no big deal."

"You never know with some people," says Archie darkly, wagging his finger at me. "She's American, she's into sport. They're the ones to watch. Haven't you watched any American high-school dramas?"

I sigh. "She was okay with you, wasn't she?"

"Well, of course she was, no one can fight my natural charm. Anyway, it's not like I've got *GAY* written in neon capital letters on my forehead, is it?"

"Oh, really?" I reach up on tiptoes and trace the letters on Archie's forehead. "Come on, we'll be late for class."

JOSH

Monday evening. I've been waiting for the right time. I hardly need to check the photo, as the name of the fertility clinic is burned into my mind.

I shut my bedroom door and keep my music on low, so that I can hear if anyone's coming. I told Mum and Ima I was doing my homework, so they shouldn't disturb me. My screen is tilted away from the door.

I pause for a moment. I wonder what Becky would think. She's always said she doesn't want to know about the donor, isn't interested in him, but I think that's just her being loyal to Mum and Ima. I bet she does really, deep down. If I actually found him, I'm sure she'd change her mind.

I've already checked out the official websites, the registries and the databases, but, without your parents' consent, there's nothing you can see until you're at least sixteen. But now I've got the name of the fertility clinic, I bet I can find out more. There must be another way. There's always another way.

I don't know what I expect to find there, but the fertility clinic website is useless. It's just a business selling its services. There's nothing about children at all, just sperm and embryos and babies – nothing about what happens afterwards.

Eventually, after scrolling through a lot of rubbish on Google, I find a list with links to donor profiles, whatever they are. I click on the fertility clinic name and the year, and a table appears. My heart's beating really fast now. Each item on the list has a number and next to that a brief description – height, weight, job, eye colour, date of donation last used.

There are so many and one of them, surely, must be my dad. Not just a number. A real person.

But I'm no closer to finding him. How on earth could I work out which of these donors was the one that Mum and Ima used? The list goes on and on – how did they ever choose?

I look at the column headings again. *Date of donation last used.*

The *last* time? Which means that each donor's sperm must have been used many times over many years. So it wouldn't just be Mum and Ima who chose this donor, but other people could have chosen him too.

Which must mean that we could have brothers and sisters all over the world. Little ones and older ones. Each one as closely related to Becky and me as we are to each other. Different mothers, same dad. All out there somewhere, maybe loads of them, all in different families and perhaps even different countries. And we don't know who or where or how to find out more about them.

It's not just me and Becky, the way it's always been. It's not just the two of us any more. This is immense. I thought it was just about finding my dad. But now it's bigger than that. Instead of getting closer to the truth, I feel like there's even more I don't know. It makes me dizzy just thinking about it.

I need to know more, so I go back to searching, flicking from page to page, but there's nothing here for me. It's all about waiting till you're older. But I don't want to wait.

There are groups and message boards for parents, or people thinking about becoming parents, discussing the choices they are making. I skim through these for a while, but it's all boring. Each person who posts just wants everyone else to agree with them.

Then there are websites for adults who call themselves "DC" – donor-conceived. Most are DC because their parents couldn't have biological kids for medical reasons, some have single mums, and some, like us, have gay parents. But they are all ancient, in their twenties or much older, talking about how they found out by accident or didn't know until they grew up. When they were teenagers, most of them didn't even know they were donor-conceived. What good is that to me?

Finally, I find a link to a secret online group for "younger" donor-conceived kids. But younger than what? There's no age mentioned, but I bet they are not going to let a thirteen year old join, not without asking questions first.

I don't want to stop now. I check the door's definitely shut and start by creating a profile that makes it look like I'm sixteen, with a date of birth three years before my real one. Next, I send an email about myself to the group admin. It's true, but with a few details changed. I try to make it friendly, but not too friendly, and vague enough that it won't make people ask any awkward questions.

I read it over, once, twice, then hit *send* before I can change my mind.

My mouth is dry with nerves. This isn't me. Becky was always the one who was good at making up stories or ideas for let's-pretend games, not me. When we were little, if something was broken or spilled or missing, Mum and Ima would always ask me what had happened before they asked Becky. They knew I was a rubbish liar. I didn't see the point. It always made me feel twisted up inside. They'd find out the truth soon enough anyway, so why try to hide it?

I stare at my inbox, then hit refresh a few times.

Come on.

Nothing.

After pacing around for a bit, I hear a thump on the landing outside my bedroom. Then another. I shove my phone in my pocket and open the door to see what's going on.

I nearly trip over a pile of black bin bags and dusty cardboard boxes. Straight ahead I can see Mum's legs at the top of the ladder sticking out of the loft hatch.

I jump back as another box comes flying down and lands with a thud exactly where my toes had been a second before. The legs start moving downwards, gradually revealing the rest of Mum. She has her hair tied back and she's wearing her oldest clothes, the ones normally saved for gardening or painting the shed. She looks both determined and pleased with herself.

"Goodness, it needs a sort out up there. It really does." She wipes her hands on her jeans, leaving faint grey smears.

"Is that what you're doing?" I ask. "Sorting out the attic?" I poke at one of the bags with my toe and a cloud of dust rises. "What are you going to do with all this stuff? It looks ancient."

"It's all got to go. There's no point in keeping all this clutter."

"What?" Suddenly Becky is barrelling up the stairs at top speed. She has a superhuman sixth sense which alerts her when anything is about to be thrown away. "What's got to go? What do you mean?"

"It's not your stuff, Becks, don't worry. Just some old clothes I'm never going to wear again and old notes from college I'm never going to read again. Nothing we need to keep."

I can tell Becky's still suspicious. She sits down on the floor and starts to rip tape off one of the boxes.

"Stop it," insists Mum, pushing the box out of her reach.

"Look, if you're so bothered, why not go up into the attic yourself and look at all the boxes of *your* things that I'm *not* throwing away?"

"All right then, I will."

When Becky's halfway up the ladder, Mum says softly, "At least, I'm not throwing them away *yet*."

"I heard that!" shouts Becky.

Mum raises her eyebrows at me and smiles, like we're in on a secret together. I smile back briefly, then turn away. I don't want Mum to meet my eyes or I might end up blurting out my own secrets.

After a moment, she says, "I suppose I'd better get these boxes downstairs. Will you give me a hand, Josh?"

"Er, in a minute… I'd like to go and have a look at what's in the attic first."

"Okay then, go on. Make sure you turn the light out when you and Becky come down though, and shut the hatch properly. Oh, and watch where you step on those old boards. No jumping up and down or clog-dancing or anything like that." She grabs two bulging bin bags and heads down the stairs.

There's a single bare bulb in the attic, which casts strange shadows and makes it hard to work out what's where or how big the space is. Some boxes are neatly packed and labelled, others are overflowing, the contents all mixed up. Becky's perched on an old suitcase, flicking through a pile of children's books.

"Look, our books!" she exclaims. "She mustn't ever get rid of *any* of these. Remember how you used to love these *Topsy and Tim* books?"

"You did too," I reply. "You were always trying to get me to act them out with you, or you were making up new adventures…"

"With me as Topsy and you as Tim!" Becky adds.

Just watching her leaf through the books reminds me of the smell of our old bedroom, me under my blue stripy duvet, Becky with her teddy Mr Snuffles, and Ima reading us both stories before she and Mum tucked us up in bed for the night.

I peer into a box. It's full of glass jars from the time Ima got into jam-making and the kitchen always smelled of boiling fruit. Next to it are a couple of bags of our old primary school uniforms and some faded pictures in ugly frames. I'm surprised Mum hasn't got rid of these already.

"Do you think it's because she's going to be fifty?" asks Becky. "All this clearing and sorting. Like she's spring-cleaning her life or something."

"Hmm, maybe." That sounds a bit too deep. "More

likely she just got fed up with all this junk. I mean, if you sorted out this place properly, you could have a whole other room up here. That'd be great, wouldn't it?" An alternative view of the attic starts to take shape in my mind. "I know, it could be a games room. You could fit in a pool table, no problem. Table football too."

"Yeah, that would be pretty cool, I guess. But where would we put all our stuff then?"

"Obvious – chuck it."

She grabs a pair of old socks from a school-uniform bag and throws them at me. "Shut up, it's our history, isn't it? We can't just chuck it away."

"But you can't live in the past, can you? Better to turn this room into something useful." I tuck the socks neatly back in the bag again.

Becky snorts, and turns back to looking through the books, as if to say, *Conversation over.*

There *is* some interesting stuff up here. But something about it is unsettling too. All the things that used to be new and shiny and fresh, now sitting unused and forgotten. Tiny bits of dust hovering in the air, caught in the beam of the light bulb.

There's a long silence and then I have to say it.

"If you're so into our history and remembering

everything, then why aren't you interested in finding him? I just don't get it."

She knows what I mean straight away.

"I…I don't know. Maybe because *this* is our history, this is who we are." She looks around. "All of this mess and muddle. It's ours. It's nothing to do with some guy I've never met. The donor hasn't been there for all of this – and that's okay. Like Mum says, that's not what he signed up to do. Mum and Ima do my head in sometimes, but *they're* our family, not some stranger." She looks up at me, eyes concerned. "Sorry, Josh."

"But not knowing – doesn't it bother you?" I insist. "You wouldn't have to meet him. Don't you want to know something about him though? I mean, it could even be someone you know, someone you walk past every day?" I pause, then try out my new idea on her. "What if we've got sisters or brothers out there somewhere?"

But she doesn't take it seriously.

"Ha, one brother's enough for me, thanks. Anyway, if you want to start finding out, it's easy, just ask Mum and Ima. Why not? Or wait till you're sixteen, then you can apply to find out loads of stuff about him. It's not that long."

"Because…oh, I don't know…*how* would I ask them?

It feels kind of rude, like I'm being ungrateful. I don't know what I'd say, what they'd say. And if they wanted us to know, they'd have told us, wouldn't they? They'd at least talk about it or ask us if we'd like to know. But no one says anything. It's this big unspoken thing."

"It's only big to you. If it matters that much, just talk to them about it. If you mentioned it, then it wouldn't be unspoken, would it?" Becky looks pleased with herself for thinking of this, then her expression softens. "Talk to Mum at least, you know she always listens."

Becky's making sense. I can't argue with her, which is annoying. I know that she's right. It *would* be much easier just to talk to Mum, or even to Ima, instead of sneaking around.

And yet. What if I did ask and they said they *didn't* want to help me find my dad, or they were angry, or upset? Surely it's better to do my own detective work and not worry them for no reason. I'll tell them once there's something to tell.

"Hey there, earth calling Josh!" says Becky gently. I snap back out of my dream. She looks at me anxiously. "Look, you can talk to me, right? So why's it so hard to talk to Mum and Ima?"

"But that's you, Becky. That's different."

"Yeah." She nods. "I know, it's always been different with us. But I could talk to them for you?"

"No!" I snap. "No…" I say again, more calmly this time. "Thanks, Becks, but…"

I stop because I can feel my pocket buzzing. I turn away from Becky as I pull out my phone.

One new notification. From the DC group.

BECKY

It feels like Carli's been at Larkhall for ever.

She fits in so easily. It's hard to describe, it's like there was always a space waiting for her, but we hadn't noticed it was there until she arrived to fill it. She seems to get on with everyone too. Not just the sporty kids or the clever ones or the arty ones like me and Archie – she's one of those people who has what Ima calls "a gift for friendship". I'd never really got what that meant before. I knew you could have a gift for art or music or even maths – but friendship? But now I've met Carli, I know just what Ima's talking about.

I wake up on Friday morning with a good feeling inside. It lasts all through the day. Nothing spoils it – not even Josh acting weird on the way in, checking his phone every five seconds, or a surprise maths test just before lunch or the horrible drizzly weather.

I hold this feeling all day like a secret hugged close to my chest. I feel like I did on the first day of term: like something special's just about to happen.

It's good, in a way, that Josh is so distracted right now, because I'm not ready to share how I'm feeling with him, or anyone. If I did, then I'd have to try and explain it, and I can't, not yet. Not even to Josh…not even to myself.

Carli and I have different lessons at the end of the day, so we've arranged to meet by the gates so that she can walk home with me. By the time I get out of school, I can see she's already there waiting. My stomach feels jittery but I don't know why. Perhaps I shouldn't have finished off Archie's leftover chips at lunchtime.

"Come on, let's go," she says, grabbing my arm and tucking herself close in beside me so that she can shelter under my umbrella. "What *is* this weather?"

"Oh, so it never rains in America?" I tease.

"In Arizona, not so much. We have deserts. It's, like, ninety-five degrees or something in the summer. It was getting pretty hot already when we left last month."

"What's ninety-five degrees?"

"What? Really? You don't…okay, ninety-five degrees is hot, that's all you need to know. Hotter than I can ever imagine it getting here." She sighs.

"Do you miss it? Home, I mean."

She goes quiet. I worry I've asked a stupid, obvious question.

"Yeah, and no. Like, I hadn't realized it would be so different here. We've travelled with my dad's job before, but only in the US. Here, all the schoolwork is different – half the places they talk about in geography, I've got no idea what or where they are, and history – all those kings, all with the same names. And when I say stuff, and people look at me like they have no idea what I'm talking about, like I'm just some dumb American… It's so exhausting, y'know."

I nod, trying to be understanding, but I'm blushing too. What if she's saying it about me too – what if I'm one of the people who's made her feel stupid? I try not to think about that.

"But then, I thought starting school mid-semester would be hard, and it wasn't. Meeting Archie and you and everyone – well, maybe it's silly, but I feel like I *am* at home now. Like I've known you all for ever, even though it's just been a few days. That's been so cool."

"I know what you mean. It feels loads more than two weeks since term started. This week's been so long…"

"But now it's the weekend!"

"I love Fridays, knowing you've got two whole days to do whatever you like." A memory pops into my head. I want to tell Carli everything and anything, even silly stuff from when I was little that only Archie or Josh know. "In Reception, we had this teacher, Miss Patel – she was the best. She had this special song she always got us to sing on Fridays. We used to go wild about it."

"Oh yeah? You gonna teach it to me then?"

"What, me? Now?"

"Yes, of course you. Miss Patel's not here, is she?"

"Okay then, but I warn you, I'm not the best singer… and it's a bit babyish really… I mean, we were only five or something…"

"Becky!" She's staring at me. This is a challenge.

"Okay, it goes like this – 'Friday's here, Friday's here, let's all give a great big cheer!'" I glance up and she's looking straight at me, amused.

"Hey, don't stop…" she says. "I know that tune. The real words are 'This old man' or something, aren't they?"

"Okay." I sound grudging, but I'm actually enjoying it. "'1, 2, 3, 4, 5, Friday's so much fun, what a shame

67

there's only one – till…next…week!'"

"I love it. I can just imagine you as a little kid singing it too. Let me try."

And then she starts singing, not shy at all. I look around and then think, *Who cares?* and join in. By the time we turn into my road, we're both singing at the tops of our voices.

An old woman pulling a wheelie shopping trolley gives us a disapproving look as we pass her, clocking the badges on our blazers in case she decides to complain to the school about our behaviour. When she's gone, Carli imitates her sour face so perfectly that I burst out laughing.

"You are so embarrassing!" I tell her as I unlock the front door.

"That's why you love me!" she retorts.

My breath catches. What does she mean by that?

"Come on then, why are we standing outside? Let's go in."

It probably meant nothing, I decide, just one of those things people say. I step back so Carli's first through the door.

As I follow her inside, I can smell something delicious in the slow cooker. Mum always puts Friday night dinner on to cook in the morning before work. There's no sign of Josh, so I guess Carli and I are the first ones home. But it won't be long until Mum and Ima are back and I still haven't said anything to Carli. I told Archie that it didn't worry me, telling Carli about my mums, but even so, I've been putting it off.

She kicks off her shoes, leaving her bag next to mine by the door, and wanders through to the living room.

"So when do your mom and dad get back?" she asks, looking around. "Will they like me, do you think?"

"Course they'll like you," I say quickly and take a deep breath. "But I haven't got a dad."

"Oh, I'm sorry." A little wrinkle appears on Carli's forehead, which I know by now means something's confusing her. "But you always talk about your parents, so I thought…did they split up then?"

"No, no, nothing like that. I mean, I've never had a dad – I've got two mums."

"*Two* moms?" I'm used to this, watching people's faces to see what they are thinking, waiting while they work it through in their heads and then for the penny to drop once they realize what I mean.

"My mums are gay," I add, in case Carli needs a bit of extra help in working this one out.

"That's so cool," she says at last. "I've never had a

69

friend with gay parents. I just didn't expect it, that's all. My family's so boring. Wait till you meet my mom and dad. I wish I wasn't an only child – then at least there'd be someone else around to make things more exciting. Perhaps my mom and dad would be more chilled out if I had a brother or sister, like you've got Josh."

I breathe a sigh of relief. Now that's done. She didn't say anything awful or run a mile or anything. I mean, I didn't think she would, not really, but... Now I just hope she's not going to go on about it, that she's not going to ask The Question. I'm about to sweep her upstairs to my room when she starts up again.

"Becky, can I ask one thing though…?" Oh no, she is, she's going to ask which mum is my real one.

"Sure." I nod, but I've tensed up. I hate it when people ask this. I know what they want to know: who gave birth to me? Who's my biological mum? But if I say Ima's my "real" mum, then what does that make Mum? And what about Josh – is he not my "real" brother? It makes me wonder if people just see our family as a flimsy, made-up thing, not like a proper family at all.

But instead, Carli says, "What should I call your moms? Are they both Mrs Silverman?"

I laugh with relief. "No, don't call either of them Mrs

Silverman! Mum's not a Silverman anyway, even though the rest of us are. You can just call them by their names – Ruth and Anna."

"What do *you* call them though? Doesn't it get confusing to call them both Mom – I mean, Mum?"

"Yeah, they thought of that. There's Mum and then there's Ima…"

"Ima?"

"It's Hebrew for Mum," I explain.

"Why Hebrew?"

"Oh, Ima's side of the family come from Israel. They came to live over here when she was a teenager. We're Jewish. Well, Mum didn't start out Jewish, but when she met Ima she started going to synagogue too, and…"

I look up. Carli's staring at me. I tail off, embarrassed. I bet now she thinks I'm really weird. I mean, not only have I got gay parents, but religious ones too.

Carli carries on looking straight at me, then she says, "Becky Silverman, you are one of the most interesting people I know."

This makes me glow, I can't help it.

But I don't want Carli to think the only reason I'm interesting is because of my family. I want her to think I'm interesting because I'm me.

"But, well, I didn't think you *could* be gay and religious. I mean my mom says…" She tails off. "Maybe it's different if you're Jewish. Sorry, I guess it's a stupid question."

"No, it's not stupid. Some Jewish people think it's not okay to be gay – but not all of them. Our synagogue's really cool about it. They fly a rainbow flag at Pride and everything. Ima always goes on at us about how being Jewish isn't about following rules, it's about working together to make the world a better place for everyone."

"That's awesome. There's no way our church back home would fly a rainbow flag! It's nothing like your synagogue. It's really traditional. Just like my mom and dad."

She stops, as if wondering whether or not to go on. "I mean, there's lots of things they don't approve of. Like, well, like gay marriage and stuff…"

I feel myself going red.

"But I don't agree…" continues Carli anxiously. "I mean, I don't agree with them, not I don't agree with gay marriage."

It's the first time I've seen Carli look flustered.

"It's okay," I say, wishing we could talk about something else. "Really."

"You're sure?"

I nod.

"Both Mom and Dad are quite protective," she goes on. "I'm their little girl. It took some persuading for them to let me come round tonight at all… They'll probably message me in a minute just to check I wasn't abducted on the way back to your house!" She smiles, but I can tell it bothers her. "You can imagine what they said when I got this!" She pushes back her hair and points to the silver hoop at the top of her ear and raises her eyebrows.

"I'm just lucky." I shrug. "Josh and I look after ourselves when Mum and Ima are working – Mum's a nurse and Ima manages an old people's home, so they often work shifts. It's always been like that. They trust us not to do anything stupid. Well, they trust Josh mainly. He's the sensible one. I guess you're right though – because there's two of us, it makes it okay."

"Your mums sound so cool. Like I said, my parents are always on my case." Carli sighs as she continues to explore the living room.

"Hey, is this them?" she asks suddenly, picking up a framed photo balanced on the edge of one of the cluttered shelves. I nod. I'm glad she spotted that one. I'm really proud of that picture. I caught them both leaning into each other, sharing a joke at my cousin's wedding. Mum's brushing Ima's dark curly hair away from her eyes. They look so relaxed and happy.

"So who's who?"

"This is Mum. You can call her Anna." I point. "And this is Ima. She's Ruth."

"Wow, she's got such beautiful hair. Just like yours."

"Yeah, well," I mutter.

"It's true," she insists, looking up at me. "Did you take this? It's such a good photo."

I nod. "Do you want to see some more?"

We sit on the sofa, and I show her my latest photography club project on my tablet. She seems really interested, asking questions about the light or why I chose to take a certain shot, even spotting things in the background that I hadn't noticed before. By the time we start looking at my favourite photographers – Rena Effendi, Dorothy Bohm – online, my worries about boring her have slipped away.

I'm so absorbed that I hardly notice the sound of the front door opening. But Carli does.

"C'mon then." She throws my tablet down on the sofa. "Let's go meet your moms."

JOSH

From my bedroom upstairs, I hear the front door open, then slam shut. I stay still. If I keep quiet enough, Becky won't realize I'm here. Then I'll have more time to try and work this out.

There's a murmur of voices. It confuses me for a second – surely Mum and Ima aren't home yet – then I realize Carli's here. Of course, it's Friday.

Becky and Carli have been together all week: arm in arm through the corridors, messaging all the time. It's even shut Archie up. At first, he was even louder and more over-the-top than usual, but now he just looks a bit…lost. Still, Becky will work it out. She always does. She's always been good at making friends. And I like Carli too: she's funny, friendly, she's even into football.

I bet if she tried out for the girls' team at Larkhall, she'd get in.

If I put as much effort into homework as I have into finding my dad, Ima and Mum would be over the moon. I haven't posted anything in the private online forum I found, but now that I've got access, I've spent ages reading through other people's posts. It feels different, knowing I'm not alone. It's strange to think that there are people out there asking the same questions, feeling the same gap that I do, and that some of them have even found brothers and sisters already. And if they can find them, then surely I could too.

My mind is buzzing. All I've been able to think about these last few days is how my dad, or even a brother or a sister, could be searching for me too. Perhaps they are looking for me right now. They could be on the other side of the world or just round the corner. They could even be in this DC group or have posted on one of the other sites I've visited. They could be so close without me even knowing it.

There's no space left in my mind to think about school, or Mum's surprise party or anything else. Jayden asked if I was playing football tomorrow, but I couldn't even be bothered to answer. Archie said something about posters for the Pride group, but I didn't really listen. Even the smell of dinner cooking downstairs doesn't make me feel hungry.

I scroll my way through the forum again, looking at photos, rereading messages, and click on a new post from this guy called Eli. He's posted before, about how his mum is always going on about him being donor-conceived and how sometimes he just wants to forget about it and be like everyone else. This time he's posted a link to an article, with an embarrassed emoji next to it and the message *Look what she's done now!* Underneath in the comments are lots of thumbs ups, exclamation marks and smiley faces.

The article's about Eli's mum – well, not just her, there are other families interviewed too. It's really gushy – *Claire Armistead invites me into the home she shares with her son Elijah, 16, in the outskirts of Manchester*, it begins. *Like any proud parent, she doesn't need asking twice to start talking about her family, but this is a family with a difference…* And so it goes on.

The title's *One Big Happy Family* – which is a bit corny – but the pictures of the different families are really good. Even Becky would be impressed with these.

I think Eli's brave to share this article. It's pretty

personal stuff. I can feel myself cringing on his behalf. I'd hate it if Mum and Ima told the world all about our family life – but I don't think they ever would.

Then I scroll down further, and my heart stops.

On the screen is a photo of me.

No, not me, not quite, not now. But me how I imagine I'll look when I'm sixteen or seventeen.

I reach out to touch the screen, tracing the outline of Eli's face just to check. There's my dark hair, my freckles, my eyes. Even the angle of his front tooth is the same as mine. Could it be true? Could this Eli be my brother?

A loud laugh from downstairs makes me jump. I check my watch. It's already well after six – I must have lost track of time. Mum and Ima will be wondering where I am.

I can't stop myself having one more look at the screen before I go down. This time it's not quite so obvious that we look the same. So I look again, zoom in closer, remind myself of the features that were so obvious just a few minutes before. Yes, I tell myself, *yes*, there they are. Of course they are. The eyes, hair, that crooked front tooth. Yes. So what now?

I slip quietly out of my room and down the stairs. In the kitchen, I hear Carli asking how she can help and Ima explaining where to find the plates.

I pause on the bottom step. Everything downstairs is bright and light, no shadows, no secrets. For Becky, Ima and Mum, nothing has changed since I saw them this morning. But will they notice anything different about me?

I slowly push open the door.

Ima breaks off from her explanation of what's in which cupboard and looks up. "Oh, there you are, Josh. Have you been in all this time?"

"Yeah, just upstairs. Sorry, forgot the time."

"What? I didn't even know you were here," squeals Becky. Her face is flushed and she's talking more loudly than usual. "What've you been doing up there that's so secret?"

"None of your business," I snap. "I'm here now, aren't I?"

"I bet you were just hiding until *we'd* got everything ready, so then you could just turn up and eat. That's so rude."

"Shut up, Becky. You don't know anything."

"Come on, you two, remember we have a guest," says Mum firmly, which is her way of saying *Stop arguing now or else*. She pushes glasses into my hands, and knives and forks into Becky's, steering us towards the table. Carli's already neatly laying out the plates, chatting with Ima. It's like she's always here on Friday nights, instead of visiting for the first time.

The thought of maybe having a brother somewhere out there has shaken me up, plus everything Becky says or does is really getting on my nerves tonight. Yet, despite that, I still relax. I love Friday nights. Always have. Mum and Ima both work evenings sometimes, but Friday's the one night they are both always here. We sit round the table, we turn the TV off, we even use the nice tablecloth that Ima says came from her grandparents. We don't do anything religious, except for Ima lighting the candles to welcome in Shabbat, but it still feels special.

"You have such a beautiful home." Carli beams as we sit down.

I didn't think anyone outside of films said things like that, even Americans. But the way she says it makes it sound like more than just some nice polite words. It's like she really means it. Ima smiles broadly.

I look round, trying to see our house as if for the first time – *do* we have a beautiful home? It's messy, colourful, but not like anything you'd see in one of those glossy magazines that they have in the dentist's waiting room. There are embarrassing old photos of me and Becky, splodges of paint samples on the wall with the names of the colours scrawled next to them, piles of books on the floor from when the shelf collapsed, which no one's bothered to fix yet.

But my thoughts can't help drifting back to Eli. Could he really be my big brother? I want to believe it so much. *Brother* – I turn the word over in my mind, and then tuck it away again, something special to explore later.

"I hope you're not a vegetarian, Carli," Ima says, as she ladles chicken casserole onto our plates. Carli shakes her head. "Good, that's a relief. Becky's told us lots about you, but I forgot to ask her what you do or don't eat. I just hope you've got a good appetite, as food's very important in this house! Now everyone just help yourselves. Don't hold back."

Once everyone's plates are piled high, Ima leans forward and starts on the questions. No one will pay attention to me for a while, so I sneak a few extra potatoes and concentrate on eating as much as I can. My appetite's never gone for long.

"So, Carli, whereabouts in the States are you from? Becky hasn't quite told us *everything* about you yet."

"Ima," moans Becky. "Just let her eat."

"It's okay," says Carli. "I'm from Tucson originally,

it's in Arizona. We've moved around a bit for my dad's job, but never lived in Europe before."

"And what does your dad do?"

"Something to do with chemical engineering. He's got, like, a year-long placement to set up this new team for the company in the UK…"

"A year!" butts in Becky. "I didn't know it was only a year."

"Well, maybe. Maybe more." Carli shrugs. "It depends how it goes, I guess."

"And your mum? Sorry, tell me if I'm being too nosy!"

Becky catches my eye and grimaces. I smile back. Ima's always like this with new people, wanting to know everything about them. Becky's the same, but she won't admit it.

"Mom's a homemaker. Oh, and she does lots of volunteer work. At least, she used to back home, I don't know what she'll do here. Dad's job's in London, but my parents wanted to live out here. They think it's safer."

"And cheaper," says Ima. "I can't believe some of the prices people pay to live in London. It's ridiculous. So where in town are you?"

"Down by the park, Cherry Avenue."

Ima's eyebrows shoot up, and she coughs with surprise.

Cherry Avenue is one of the poshest roads in town. Huge houses with long driveways and tall gates with intercoms. The smartest cars outside. Most people at our school live in ordinary streets like ours, or in the flats by the football stadium. I don't know anyone else who lives in Cherry Avenue.

It's gone unusually quiet for our house.

"This meal's delicious," says Carli, breaking the silence.

BECKY

"I'm so sorry about that," I say, once we're upstairs in my room. "The way Ima kept asking you all those questions about your family, and then all that stuff about human rights and guns and everything – like you should have an opinion on everything to do with America. Was it too full on? I thought they'd never stop." I know I'm rattling on, but I can't seem to stop talking.

Carli puts her hand on my arm to slow me down. "Hey, don't worry. I liked her. I liked both your moms, okay?"

"You're sure?"

"Course I'm sure. Anyway, I like the way everyone talks in your house – about politics, what's in the news, everything. And your moms ask you what you think, like

84

they really want to know. They treat you like adults. I can't imagine anything you say would really shock them. My parents…well, like I said, it's different. Are there any other kids at Larkhall with parents like yours?"

"Like what? Who never shut up, do you mean?" I say, deliberately misunderstanding her. I know what she really means.

"No." Carli laughs. "Sorry, I might not say it right, but, you know, anyone else with two moms or two dads?"

"Oh, no – at least I don't think so. Most people don't know about Mum and Ima, so there may be other families that we don't know about, I guess. Although, I think if there were, Archie would have found out about them by now."

"Archie?"

"Whatever the gossip is, Archie's first to know. He likes to know everything that's going on."

"Yeah, true. He told me about this Pride group he's starting next Wednesday…"

I roll my eyes. "Of course he did. Has he asked you to help put up posters? Or make cakes?"

"Yeah, how did you know? I don't mind though. It sounds cool. I guess you'll be going along…" She pauses. "I mean, what with your moms and everything. Hey, maybe there'll be someone else there whose family's like yours."

"Maybe." I mean, why shouldn't there be? Larkhall's a big enough school, after all. Thinking about it makes me feel weirdly uncomfortable, but excited too. "We do know other families with two mums – friends of Ima's and Mum's – but they don't live round here. It's not *that* unusual."

"I didn't mean your family was weird or anything."

"I know, it's okay," I say hurriedly. "Look, anyway, are you coming on Wednesday? Anyone can come, like, you don't have to be LGBTQ or anything...I mean, I'd really like you to come... But you don't have to...it might be really boring and..." I tail off.

I've started blushing, I don't know why. I cross the room to draw the curtains, so that Carli can't see my red face.

My room's small – you could barely swing a gerbil in here, let alone a cat – but it's cosy. Most of the space is taken up by my loft bed – it's like a bunk bed, but with space underneath instead of the bottom bunk – and a tiny, battered old desk under the window. There's not even enough room for my wardrobe so it sits in the hallway outside. In fact, I'm guessing the whole room must be about a quarter of the size of Carli's bedroom in Cherry Avenue.

It's getting dark, but the rain has cleared. Before I close the curtains, I spot a bright crescent moon, the sort you see in a children's picture book. I'm about to point it out to Carli, but she speaks first.

"I'd love to come," says Carli, coming up behind me. "I'd already said to Archie that I would… Oh, what's under there – can I look?"

Before I can answer, she lifts the drapes of material hanging around the sides of my loft bed and peers underneath.

We used to store all our toys underneath our beds – baskets of ponies and teddies, action figures and board games – but now all of those are up in the attic, unless Mum's thrown them away. Although Josh has replaced his loft bed with a proper one now, I still love mine. I've made the space underneath into my own hideaway place. I've covered the floor with fluffy cushions and taped tiny white fairy lights like stars to the bottom of the bed above so they sparkle down on me. Heavy deep-blue material draped round the sides blocks out most of the sound and light from outside. I sneak away in here to write my diary or call Archie or simply to be by myself. Normally I don't like anyone going in here but me – Archie's too tall anyway to fold up his long legs into such a small space. It's secret, special, but with Carli I don't mind.

"Oh wow," breathes Carli. "This is like a secret world. Can I go in?"

I crawl under the bed, quickly shoving my diary under the nearest cushion – I don't want anyone finding that – and Carli follows. There's just about space for us both to get comfortable against the cushions, but we have to squash up a bit. I'm so close that I can smell her shampoo, hear her breathing, feel her leg brush against mine. I'm glad that when Carli asked Josh after dinner if he wanted to hang out with us, he said no.

"Who's this?" says Carli, producing a faded pink teddy that she's found nestled among the cushions.

"Oh." I blush. "That's Mr Snuffles."

"Mr Snuffles? Who called him Mr Snuffles?"

"I hope you're not going to say anything rude about him." I grab the bear from her and cover his ears with my hands. "He's very sensitive."

Carli giggles. "Of course not. But is that really his name?"

"Yeah, I've had him since I was tiny. No one can remember now who named him and why. I used to take him everywhere – only when I was little of course – that's why he's so worn out. Now he just hangs out here."

"Well…" Carli turns to the bear and says very seriously, "Pleased to meet you, Mr Snuffles, I hope we're friends for a long time." She turns back from Mr Snuffles to me.

"Just you wait till you come to my house, Becky. I've still got loads of soft toys from when I was a kid. I know some people think it's babyish, but I don't care. You could bring Mr Snuffles! Of course, I had to leave some back home in storage, like this really big fluffy rabbit I've got, because we couldn't move everything over, not if we're just here for the year. We've had to buy lots of things new, but it's cool – like, we got this new TV delivered yesterday. It's huge, like being at the movies but at home. When you come over…" She breaks off, noticing how quiet I've gone. "What?"

"Nothing."

"Becky, what?"

"Oh, it's just I was thinking, I bet you've got loads of great stuff at your house, that's all. Much better than anything here."

Carli runs her hands through her short hair. I watch her, until she looks at me, and then I look away quickly.

We sit there for a little while in silence. Finally, she says quietly, "We've got lots of *new* stuff because we had to move. That doesn't make it better than what you've got. Did you think I was showing off?"

"No, but…"

"Do you think I'm stuck-up just because I live on Cherry Avenue? And, because I live in a bigger house than you do, that I won't want to be your friend?"

A tight, tense feeling is growing in my chest. "No, of course not. It's just…oh, I don't know. Let's not talk about it any more."

She looks at me hard, her blue eyes still and serious. "Okay, we won't. But first you have to promise you *will* come round my house. Not because I want to show off, but because I like hanging out with you. Okay?"

"Okay, all right." I breathe out.

"Promise?"

"Promise."

JOSH

Archie and the others have been busy. The rainbow posters are everywhere, like some kind of brightly-coloured rash has swept the school. I even helped put some of them up. Archie's hard to say no to and, you know, good luck to him and everything.

"You're not really going, are you?" asks Max on Wednesday lunchtime, as the bell rings for the end of geography.

"What?"

"You know, this group, this gay thing? Not seriously."

"Yeah, why not? It's just like a club, it's for anyone, it's…" I stop. I actually have no idea what's going to happen at the Pride group this lunchtime. I just said I'd go along to shut Archie up, and because Becky would

91

probably have had a go if I didn't. I remember another reason too. "Anyway, there's cake."

"What's this?" says Jayden, coming up behind us and giving me a punch on the arm. It doesn't hurt, it's just annoying. "Turning gay on us, Josh? We'd better watch out." He sniggers.

"No, don't be stupid."

"I know why he's really going…" says Max.

"Oh yeah?"

"He's after Carli, that's why. I've seen her putting up some of those posters…"

"What, Carli's a lez? No way, what a waste," butts in Jayden, shaking his head. Then he thinks for a moment. "Still, my dad says any girl who's that into sport must be gay. I mean, netball and all of that, that's okay for girls, it's not a proper sport anyway, but football, well, you've seen some of those girls on the England team, they're just like blokes…"

I've learned to tune out and just nod once Jayden starts telling us what his dad says about things. It's usually rubbish.

"Carli doesn't look like a bloke," protests Max. "Anyway, she says she's just helping out. Whatever, I reckon Josh fancies her." He turns to me. "Heard she was round your house on Friday."

"That's just cos she's friends with Becky, that's all."

"You sure that's all?" says Jayden, doing that punch thing on my arm again. I think he's copied it from his brother, who's one of the toughest kids in Year Eleven, always shoving past everyone else in the corridors and swearing loudly. Whenever we get a new teacher, they raise their eyebrows when they hear Jayden's last name and ask, with a sigh, if he's Danny Andrews's brother.

That makes me think about Eli. Since seeing his picture in that article, I've gone back and reread all his posts, looking for signs that he might really be my brother. He sounds cool, nothing like Jayden's big brother. Although, whatever he's like, I don't care – having any kind of big brother would be amazing. I'd no longer be the only guy in my family.

"Hey, wake up, Josh!" Max snaps his fingers in front of my face. "What you dreaming about? Is it your girlfriend?"

"Ah, shut up, both of you. I'd much rather spend lunchtime at the Pride group than with you pair of jokers anyway."

I can hear them laughing and catcalling as I go.

The meeting's in Ms Bryant's classroom on the ground floor, but nothing's started by the time I get there. There's a rainbow flag over the door so no one can see in from outside and, as promised, there is cake. I help myself to a rainbow cupcake and sit down.

Archie's buzzing around anxiously, there are a couple of Year Elevens spreading out some big sheets of flip-chart paper, and Ms Bryant is sitting in the corner with a pile of books to mark. I look around and wonder why Becky's not here yet.

Gradually, people start drifting in – mostly students from other years who I don't know or have only seen around. Then Carli arrives with Becky, and she flashes me her huge smile.

"Move up," says Becky and they both squeeze in next to me.

Just as Ms Bryant stands up to get things started, Becky reaches over, grabs the icing I've been saving from my cupcake, and pops it into her mouth.

"Oi, get your own," I whisper, but it's too late. We've always had to share everything at home, so I think Becky will always see my things as belonging to her too.

"So, this is *your* group," Ms Bryant says. "Not mine, not the school's, so it's up to *you* what you decide to do. I'm just here to support you, and feed anything you need back to the rest of the staff and the governors. It's really

Alex and Kris" – she gestures to the Year Elevens – "who've made this happen. We hope this LGBTQ group will be a safe and supportive space for all of you, whether you are lesbian, gay, bi, trans, questioning or queer, or simply here for your friends or families." Archie glows.

Next, we do this game where you throw a ball of wool around (rainbow wool, of course) and you have to say your name, your pronouns, and something about yourself each time you catch it.

No one asks who's LGBTQ or not, which is a bit weird seeing as we're all at an LGBTQ group, although some people say that they are when they catch the ball. You can tell everyone's looking though and wondering.

Becky and I didn't talk before the group about whether we'd say about Mum and Ima. But then we haven't talked about anything much lately. Normally we don't have to, I just kind of know what she's thinking. Not in any freaky, supernatural way, just because we're together so much.

But today it's different. I'm not sure what she's thinking. I look over at her, but she's too busy whispering to Carli. Archie knows about our mums anyway, and so does Carli and probably a few others, so I don't suppose it matters, not here at least. I don't mind people knowing – even Jayden and Max, who seem to forget all the time anyway and still say stupid things. It's not a big deal, having two mums, it's just how things are.

The game's a bit childish, but does get quite funny, as some people say really outrageous things, and others throw the ball too fast or drop it or get tongue-tied and start giggling. Before long, we're all in a huge tangle of wool.

The first time I catch the ball, I stutter and say that I'm on the football team, promising myself that next time I'll tell everyone about having two mums. But Becky beats me to it. She explains first time round. I see a few people nodding or looking surprised or even relieved, like now they know where Becky and I fit.

Then Alex starts talking about ground rules, about confidentiality and respecting each other, and Kris writes everything down (just in ordinary pen, not rainbow colours) on one of the big flip-chart pages. It's obvious how much they are enjoying being important, but even so, no one makes fun of them. I guess it's because we've chosen to be there, and because we know Ms Bryant's sat in the corner, pretending not to listen.

We gather round the final bit of paper. "Now we need to work out what we want to do in the group," says Alex. "We can write down all the ideas, then decide what we want to do first."

There's an awkward silence. All the chat has evaporated, and everyone just stares at the paper, like they are waiting for ideas to write themselves on there by magic.

"We could make badges," volunteers Kai, a friend of Alex's. "We could sell them, or just wear them, I guess." Their bag is already covered in loads of badges saying things like *Trans Power*, *They/Them* and *Queer*. I've seen Kai around before, but now, thanks to the ball-of-wool game, I know who they are.

"That's great, Kai, brilliant," gushes Alex. He carefully writes *Make badges* on the paper.

"We could do a display," says someone else. "Famous gay people in history."

"And famous trans people," chips in Kris.

"And bi," adds Carli.

Queer icons display, writes Alex, and everyone seems to be happy with that.

Now the ideas are coming fast – faster than Alex can write them down. Cake sales, speakers, an assembly, watching films. Everyone seems to have something to say. Except me.

I'm struggling even to listen. Ever since Friday night, my head's been full of Eli. I must have read that article a hundred times. I don't even mind the bit where his mum explains how they haven't traced the donor yet. If Eli *is* my brother, maybe he and I could get in touch with our donor together. It would be amazing if finding a brother could help me find my dad too.

This is wild. Way more than I dreamed possible. From knowing nothing, to maybe discovering a real-life brother – okay, half-brother – in just a few days. Finding the invoice in the filing cabinet, then the online forum, then…a brother? Not on the other side of the world, but living only a few hours from Watford. It's unlikely, I know that, but that doesn't mean it's not true. I mean, other people have found brothers and sisters online, I know they have. Just because I don't have actual evidence, documents that show Eli and I have the same donor, doesn't stop me hoping that it's true. But to be totally sure, I need to actually meet Eli for myself.

My brother Eli – I try it out, how that sounds in my head. *Eli or Elijah?* I wonder.

In my mind I plan the message I'm going to send him: *I've seen the article, I'm part of the forum, I was donor-conceived too, I wondered if we could share experiences, I've got some questions…*

But would I have the courage to send it? Perhaps I

should just wait three years till I'm sixteen before trying to find out more? Or I should at least talk to Mum and Ima about it first?

But no, I've been through all of that in my mind already too many times. It's up to me to do something. Now.

I zone back in just as Alex is rolling up the flip-chart paper and everyone is talking excitedly about plans for an LGBTQ assembly at the end of term. Becky and Carli leave together, with a wave to Archie, who's helping pack up, and I hear Carli talking about how cool the group is and how they'd never have had anything like this at her last school.

I'm one of the last to leave. I'm still there when Kris takes the rainbow flag down from the back of the door, revealing all the cheesy inspirational quotes that Ms Bryant has printed out and stuck there.

FEEL THE FEAR AND DO IT ANYWAY says the one in the centre, the curly letters accompanying a picture of someone about to bungee-jump off a bridge.

"Okay," I say to the jumper (under my breath, so no one thinks it's weird that I'm talking to the door). "Okay then, if you can be brave, then so can I."

BECKY

"**S**o, I was thinking..." says Carli, as we turn the corner into Cherry Avenue. I know we're nearly there even before I see the street sign, because the roads keep getting wider and the houses keep getting bigger. "You know how I said my parents are quite traditional?"

"Yeah?"

"Well, maybe it's better we don't tell my mom exactly what we're making the cookies for. Just say it's for some friends or something..."

"Oh," I say, surprised. "Oh, okay."

Carli was the first to volunteer at the end of last week's Pride group to bake something for this week's meeting, and it was her idea that I come round her house the night before to help.

100

"And, er, maybe don't mention you've got two moms." She looks uneasy. "Just not the first time you meet her."

"Yeah, okay." I shrug. I don't normally talk about Mum and Ima until I get to know someone anyway, but it feels weird to have someone else, even if it's Carli, telling me I shouldn't. But I've no time to worry about it, because all of a sudden, Carli grabs my arm.

"This is it!" she says. "I'm so excited you're really here."

Carli's house is small compared to some of the others, tucked away at the end of the street. But it's still about twice the size of ours.

"Don't mind my mom, okay?" she says in a whisper as she unlocks the door.

I take off my shoes carefully as I come in, so as not to mess up the soft, cream carpet, and Carli hurries me through the living room into the enormous gleaming kitchen.

I don't know why Carli's so worried about her mum. She seems nice to me, not as old-fashioned as Carli says she is, although Carli rushes me past her so fast that I hardly get to say more than hello. She's small and everything about her is neat and pastel-coloured – it all matches, from her pumps to her earrings to her eye shadow. Totally different from Mum and Ima in their scruffy jeans and trainers.

The kitchen has one of those fancy islands in the middle, and Carli puts some music on before dashing around, opening identical-looking, shiny cupboards to collect the ingredients we need. At first, I don't want to touch anything in case I mess it up, but by the time the biscuits are in the oven and everything sticky is in the dishwasher, I've stopped worrying. Soon we're sliding in our socks on the shiny kitchen floor, giggling as we twirl around the island like little kids pretending to be ice skaters.

"Ladies, this smells delicious!" says Carli's mum, coming in so quietly that I'm mid-pirouette before I realize she's in the room. She's beaming, her smile just like Carli's. "Will I be allowed to try one? They're not all for school, are they? Just one?"

"Of course," I say, as Carli gets them out of the oven.

The three of us perch on high stools, eating the biscuits, which are warm and gooey and just as delicious as they smell. Carli's mum eats so delicately that she doesn't drop any crumbs.

Looking around, I notice that the only things on the smooth, cream walls are a huge posed studio photograph of Carli, her mum, an older man who I suppose is her dad and a couple who must be her grandparents, plus prints of quotes in pastel colours. I guess they're all Bible quotes from the fact that most of them have crosses in the background. Carli's mum sees me looking at the portrait.

"We had that taken just before we left home," she says. "It's a lovely memory to have."

"Becky's really into photography," says Carli, before I can ask about the people in the photo. "She's really good too."

"Is that so?" says Carli's mum politely.

"Yes, although I'm less into portraits, more action shots. I'd love to be a photojournalist one day." I don't say that I hate studio portraits like this, with their fake backgrounds and posed smiles.

Carli's mum beams back at me. "It's so good to finally meet you, Becky. Carli's told me all about you, and how you've made her feel so welcome at school."

"Oh, right," I say, blushing, wondering what else Carli has told her mum about me. "I mean, good."

"And you've got a twin brother, Carli says. I've always thought it must be such fun to have a twin! Not like poor Carli, all on her own," she says brightly.

"Yeah, Josh and I are twins." I pause. "Well, sort of…

I mean…" Then I realize that to explain any more will mean talking about Mum and Ima – just what Carli asked me not to do – and I grind to a halt, tongue-tied.

Carli's mum opens her mouth to ask another question, but before either of us can say any more, Carli abruptly pushes back her stool and stands up.

"Mom, we're just going up to my room now, okay?"

"Sure, sweetheart. I'm not sure when Dad will be home, but I'll call you both when it's time to eat."

Carli shuts the door behind her, leans against it and lets out a long sigh.

"It's funny, isn't it?" I say. "I was worried about you meeting my mums, and you're worried about just the same thing. They're all okay though."

"Let's talk about something more interesting," she groans, flopping down on the sofa that sits across one wall of her enormous room. I sit down next to her and lean back into the soft cushions.

"Like what?"

"I know, let's play a game."

"A game? What kind of game?"

"So…we each get three questions, but we take it in turns. Any question in the whole world, but you have to answer honestly. No secrets, no lies."

I feel nervous, but excited. "No secrets, no lies," I echo.

She puts her hand on mine to seal the promise. Her skin is smooth and warm, but it still makes me shiver.

"Shall I go first?"

"Sure."

I get the feeling Carli's played this game before. She's ready with her first question.

"If you could change one thing about your family, what would you change?"

That's easy. "I'd like it if Mum and Ima didn't have to work so much. It's not even about doing more stuff together, it would just be nice having them around, instead of having to remember about homework and school trips and everything ourselves. Although I guess it's good, kind of, that they trust us." I pause and look away. "I suppose that sounds really lazy."

"No, just funny. Like, I'd want the opposite. My mom's always in my business, checking up on me. I wish she'd give me more space."

I want to offer Carli something else, something more personal. I feel a bit bad, because it's not really my secret to tell, but I tell her anyway.

"If you'd asked Josh instead of me," I carry on, "he'd say he wants to know who our biological dad is. I mean, it doesn't bother me who the sperm donor for us was. But it really bothers him."

"Really? You don't want to know?" Carli's eyes widen. "If it was me, I'd be like Josh, I'd want to know. What if you're, I don't know, a princess or something? Or your biological dad is a movie star or a millionaire?"

"Yeah, right. Or what if he's not? He's just some guy out there, probably really boring, just like everybody else. He's nothing to do with me. It's no big deal."

"So you really don't know?"

"No, but if I want to I can find out a bit more about him when I'm sixteen, and then at eighteen, I can get in touch with him. I don't know if I will though." I want to move on now. "Did that count as your second question?"

"No, no, no. That's not fair. I've still got two left. It's you now."

"Er, okay…" I rack my brains for a good question.

We've spent the last few weeks talking about everything – the books and music we like, what's happening at school, what life was like for Carli before she came to the UK. But I want to know more, I want to know everything about her, things that no one else knows. Carli always seems so assured, so confident, so finally I ask, "What are you scared of?"

"Okay, don't laugh, I'm scared…" She hesitates. "I'm scared that people won't like me."

"What? But *everybody* likes you. You're the best person at making friends that I've ever met. Honestly."

"Still, every time we go to a new place, I start a new school, and the scariest bit is – what if everyone's already got their friends and no one wants to talk to me? No lie, Becky. Oh – and I'm scared of spiders. Yuck. We have this house by the lake where we go on vacation…"

"Wait, you have a holiday house by a lake?"

"Shut up, that's not the point. The point is, whenever we open it up for the summer, it's full of spiders scuttling around. I always make Mom go into each room first and check all the corners before I'll go in, just in case there are any hiding. Stupid, huh?"

"I don't think it's stupid – and I don't think the friends thing is stupid either." Carli smiles gratefully at me. "I'm always wishing and wondering about going to new, exciting places and seeing new things – I guess I never thought about how it could be good to have always lived in the same place."

"Now, my second question." There's a glint in her eye. "Which teacher at Larkhall do you think's the cutest?"

"Er, none of them," I say firmly.

"Nope, that's not allowed. Remember, no secrets, no lies. There's gotta be someone you think is hot. Come on, I'm new here, you have to tell me everything."

I look away. I never know how to answer questions like this. Usually I just shrug them off and try to talk about something else. But I can't do that this time. There's nowhere to hide. She's looking right at me. So I think about what the other girls in Year Eight might say.

"Well, maybe Mr Ross?" It's not exactly a lie. Not really. Just because *I* don't fancy Mr Ross doesn't mean he's not one of the most fanciable teachers, does it?

Then, before she can say or ask anything else, I blurt out my next question – the first thing which comes into my mind. "Which superpower would you rather have – the ability to fly or be invisible?"

Carli doesn't even pause to think. "Ooh, fly. One hundred per cent. Imagine how amazing it would be to go up and up and up, to see everything from above, to watch it getting smaller and smaller. And whenever I wanted to go and see my friends back home, there'd be no airports or tickets or lines, I could just take off and go."

I swallow hard. I know I shouldn't feel jealous when

Carli talks about her friends in the States, but I can't help it.

"Yeah, me too. Like that bit in *The Snowman*…" She looks at me blankly. "Never mind, it's this film that's always on at Christmas here about this boy and this magic flying snowman…" She raises her eyebrows. "Stop it!" I give her a gentle shove. "Honestly, wait till your first British Christmas, then it will all make sense. Everyone watches it."

"If you say so." She smiles, looking right into my eyes. "My last question then. If you could be anywhere in the world right now, where would you want to be?"

And I look over at Carli, stretched out like a contented cat on the sofa next to me. I think about her smile, and the way she runs her hands through her hair, and how I feel like I've known her for ever after just a few weeks. And suddenly everything makes sense.

"Here," I whisper, answering her question. "Right now, the only place I want to be is here."

There's barely any distance between us now. Before I even know what I'm doing, I lean forward and kiss her.

Everything stops for one long moment. Then…

Carli moves away quickly. I feel like giggling and crying all at once – hysterical. I can't trust myself to speak.

My face is burning. I can't look at her. Did that really just happen?

"Oh, Becky, oh, I'm sorry," she says finally, her voice soft. "I didn't know that's how you felt. Honestly, I never meant..."

My head is spinning. I didn't know that was how I felt either.

Or did I? Did I really? How *could* I not have known?

"I mean, it's cool with me that you're gay," she goes on. "It's just that I'm not. I guess I should have worked it out – what with Archie being your best friend and your moms and everything. But why didn't you just tell me?" She gasps. "Was it because of my mom? I'm not like her, you know that..."

I look up and her eyes are so concerned. I can't bear it.

"You're wrong. I'm not gay," I blurt out, almost shouting. "And leave my mums out of it, okay?"

A wave of confusion crosses her face – there's that little wrinkle on her forehead that I've grown to recognize – and then it passes.

"Oh? So you're bi. Plenty of people are bi, Becks. You know Olivia in the netball team? She's bi. It's okay, really."

Olivia? I didn't know Olivia was bi, so how on earth does Carli know? She's only been in the school for five

110

minutes, but she knows and I don't. How can Olivia be bi? Olivia who's not going out with anyone. Olivia with her long blonde hair. Olivia who always gets picked first in PE.

My head is spinning. I've just totally embarrassed myself, and probably lost Carli as a friend or as… anything, and she'll most likely tell everyone that I'm gay, and then there'll be questions and whispers at school and…

"Look, I think I'd better go," I say, standing up and smoothing out my school skirt. My hands are shaking.

"Oh." Carli's face falls. "But you've still got one more question left. And I thought you were staying for dinner. It'll be nearly ready. Please, you don't have to go."

"Well, maybe another time." I force myself to yawn. "I'm a bit tired."

"Oh…okay. Well, can we give you a ride home? You know what Mom's like, she won't let you walk back by yourself in the rain, even if it's not that dark yet."

"No, no," I say quickly. "I'll call Ima. She'll come and get me."

Carli hovers next to me while I get my phone out, like she's hoping I'll change my mind and that everything can go back to how it was just a few minutes ago.

Ima sounds puzzled, but she's happy to pick me up straight away. I think she can't resist the chance to get a peek at Carli's fancy house on Cherry Avenue. I don't care as long as she comes quickly.

I perch on the edge of the bed and pretend to check my messages. Anything so as not to catch Carli's eye or have to say anything. Eventually, Carli goes downstairs to tell her mum that I'm not staying for dinner after all, while I go to the loo.

I feel so embarrassed that I hide out in the bathroom for an extra-long time, washing my hands and face really slowly and drying them carefully on the matching fluffy towels. Checking out the huge shower and counting the fancy products along the side of the bath. Trying my best not to think about what just happened.

By the time I come out, Ima's already here. I can hear her and Carli's mum chatting at the foot of the stairs. Carli's there too, laughing at something Ima said. Then Ima peers up at me.

"Are you coming then, Becky?"

I head back into Carli's room to get my jumper and my bag, before slouching downstairs.

I shove my feet into my shoes without undoing the laces, the way that always really winds Mum up –

112

"You'll wear them out" – and just about manage to mutter my thanks to Carli's mum, and agree that it's a shame I'm not feeling so well and, yes, I hope I'll feel better soon too.

It's raining outside. Ima and I dash through the puddles, coats over our heads, to where our battered little car is parked between a Land Rover and a huge Mercedes. It reminds me of what Carli said the first time we spoke, about how Americans couldn't believe British cars were so tiny. I wonder what she'd think about our tiny Fiesta, probably the last car on earth not to have doors at the back.

I hop in through the passenger's door at the front, climb through to the back and then click the front seat into place instead of clambering in next to Ima like I'd normally do. I curl up under my coat on the back seat, woolly hat pulled down so it's almost covering my eyes.

We drive in silence for a while. I watch the paths of the raindrops down the window, slow at first and then suddenly speeding up when two droplets combine and race down together.

"So what was that about?" says Ima.

"What?"

"Come on, Becky, you know what I'm talking about."

"Nothing." I trace my finger along the glass, following

one drop right from the top, until it seems to get stuck halfway down and can't move any further.

"It's not nothing. One minute you're all 'Carli this, Carli that, Carli says' and the next you're running out of her house, barely talking to her. So something happened. What?"

"I told you – nothing." I can hear the whine in my voice. I know I sound awful, but I don't know how to return to normal. I just wish Ima would stop talking, that I wasn't trapped in the car with her, with no choice but to listen.

"She seems a lovely girl. She's finding her feet in a new country, where everything is different – I know what that's like. And she doesn't know anyone, but she's found you as a friend."

"I know that."

"What I'm saying, Becky, is don't throw this friendship away when it's hardly started." She sighs. "You don't have to tell me what you rowed about. But I can guarantee it doesn't matter. Not as much as having friends matters. Especially for her, when she's far from home."

She spots a parking space near the house and brakes sharply to slide into it. The movement dislodges the droplet I've been watching, and it races away, too fast for my finger to follow. Then it's gone.

When we get back to the house, shaking the rain off our coats and kicking off our shoes, I'm desperate to be by myself, up in my room. But Mum sticks her head out of the living-room door. The noise of laughter comes from the TV behind her.

"So what was it like?" she asks, smiling. "You're back early. Didn't you have a good evening?"

"Oh, shut up!" I shout, running up the stairs two at a time. "Shut up and leave me alone."

"Becky!" Ima shouts after me. "Don't be so rude. Come back here."

"Leave it," I hear Mum say quietly to Ima. "Leave it."

I slam my door extra hard. But even that doesn't make me feel any better.

I crawl under the bed, into the place where I always feel safe, and curl up as tight and small as I can and try to forget everything. It's no good. It just makes me think of being here with Carli. I can still smell Carli's shampoo and see her face next to mine. I bury my head in a cushion to block it out, but I can't stop myself sobbing. Big, angry, snotty sobs. I've messed everything up. Stupid, stupid, stupid. Carli won't want to have anything to do with me any more. And it's all my fault.

I get out my diary from under the cushion, but there's nothing I want to write, nothing I want to remember about today. The picture of great-great-aunt Rebecca slips out. I hold it and look at her for a long time – she looks so stylish and so full of life. She looks like someone who always had a plan. What would she do? I wonder. Because *I've* got no idea.

JOSH

I should be doing my maths homework on a Tuesday evening. That's what Ima and Mum think I'm doing in my bedroom. But I'm not. I'm doing some maths of my own instead.

The problem I have is money – not enough of it for what I need.

I'm trying to work it out. I've almost got it. I have three windows open and keep flicking between them: one with the most recent message from Eli, one with a map of Manchester city centre and a third showing train times and prices.

When Eli replied to my first message last week, I decided I had to make it easy for him, even if that made it hard for me. That was my plan. I didn't want him to find any reason not to meet me. So I sort of gave the impression that I didn't live too far away, that it wouldn't be any trouble for me just to meet him for a chat, any time really, just casual, whenever he was around. And he said yes.

All I have to do now is think logically. I've always been good at that. He suggested next Saturday. I've got to be there, but I don't know if I can afford the train fare. I've still got the money I saved from my bar mitzvah. It's mostly fivers or tenners from older relatives who don't seem to have discovered online banking yet. I've kept them tucked away in the back of a drawer, just in case. I don't think even Mum and Ima realize how much I've got.

I spread out the cash on the bed: this could be a pair of trainers or some new headphones, or it could be three hours on the train to Manchester with barely enough for a McDonald's when I get there.

I look back at the screen and notice there's a link which says *earlier trains*. I click on it just to see, and then lean forward to read more closely. I can get there at half the price, but only if I leave at 6 a.m. I'll have to hang around in Manchester a bit – well, a lot – but can still get home before it's too late. I tell myself it'll be fine.

The knock on my bedroom door makes me jump. I drop my tablet and shove the money back in the drawer.

"Yeah?"

"Josh, is it okay if I come in?"

"Sure," I say, and Ima slips into my room, closing the door quietly behind her, then perches cross-legged at the end of my bed. Ima does yoga every week. It doesn't seem to make her calmer or more zen, unfortunately, but it does mean she's much more bendy than most people's mums.

"It's so dark in here," she says, peering around. "Wouldn't you like it a bit brighter? I'll turn the light on for you, shall I?"

"No, don't bother, I'm okay." I hadn't noticed till now how dark it's getting or how heavy the rain is outside. I don't mind though. "I like it like this."

"Well, all right," she says reluctantly. "At least it's tidy. Not like your sister's. Anyway, there's something I wanted to talk to you about." She lowers her voice and leans in. "It's about the party."

"You don't have to whisper, I don't think Mum can hear you from downstairs. What's she doing anyway?"

"Watching one of those medical dramas on TV. I don't get it, you'd think she'd have enough of it all day at work."

"You know she only watches them so she can moan about how it's not like real life."

Ima waves her hands. "Anyway, I wanted to ask about the playlist. I just wondered, how's it getting on? Need any help?"

"Subtle. Are you checking up on me?"

"What if I was?"

"Well, you might be surprised. It's good actually." This is true. In between sending messages and waiting for replies, I've been adding songs to the list. Trying to find things that Mum and her friends would like, and ones with a meaning or a message. There's a lot of cheesy stuff on there, not really anything I'd listen to, but I think I've done a good job. I'm pretty pleased with myself. "Do you want to look?"

I make sure I close down the windows I was browsing on the tablet and then pass it over to Ima so she can look through the tracks.

She murmurs to herself as she scrolls through. "Yes... yes...she'll love that one... Oh, I haven't heard that for ages... This is classic, like being back in the nineties... and I can just see your mum dancing to this one..."

"Please," I say. "No embarrassing dancing at this party, okay? And no singing along."

120

"You know I can't promise that." Ima smiles, looking just like Becky. "Thanks, Josh, I mean it. I wouldn't know where to start with something like that. I know you've never been sure about this party, but thanks for rolling with it. Honestly, it's going to be great."

"Yeah, well." I shrug.

"You know the plans for the day, don't you?" I do, and Ima knows I do, but it doesn't stop her going through them yet again now the party's only a few days away. She ticks each item off on her fingers as she talks. This must be how she is at work, bossing round the staff and the old people at the home. "I take Mum out during the day. She thinks that's the treat and that we're just having a quiet family dinner in the evening. Once we're gone, Auntie Jackie arrives to help you and Becky get the decorations and the house sorted. Neil's bringing round the cake and the rest of the food about five. Everyone starts arriving from six, and you all need to be in place ready before seven when we get back. I'll text you all just before we get there. And then – ta-da! Surprise!"

"Okay, fine," I say.

"Great," she says and bounces up off the bed, as if to leave the room. Then she seems to change her mind and stops, hovering by the door.

"Oh," she says, like she's just thought of it. "One more thing. Are you inviting anyone to the party? Like Jayden or Max or any of your friends from football? You know they'd be very welcome. We'll have tons of food."

"Nah, don't think so."

"Or anyone else, maybe…someone special?" presses Ima. "Maybe a girl you'd like to invite?"

"Stop it!" I warn.

"It's just, well, you've been so preoccupied lately." She sighs. "You seem to be in a dream all the time, not like my normal down-to-earth Josh. I just wondered whether there was, you know, something – or someone – on your mind at the moment. I'm not trying to pry."

Of course Ima's noticed that my mind's been elsewhere. It's probably a good thing if she thinks I'm dreaming about some girl, instead of plotting behind her back about how I'm going to meet my brother and find my dad. I'm not going to lie to her, but it won't make any difference. Once she gets an idea in her head, it won't budge. The more I deny it, the more she'll think it's true.

"There's not 'someone special'." I draw the quote marks in the air. "And even if there was 'someone special', the last thing I'd do is bring them to my mum's fiftieth birthday party to meet my entire family plus loads of old people, who've all had too much to drink and will be laughing too loudly, dancing badly and asking us when we're going to get married. Okay?"

"Okay, point taken." She lowers her voice again. "What do you reckon to this Carli then?"

I shrug. "Yeah, she's nice, I suppose. Everyone seems to like her. Talks nearly as much as Becky though."

"Everyone likes her. And you? Do *you* like her?"

"If you mean do I fancy her, then no, I don't. Leave it out, Ima. And anyway..." I trail off. I can't find the words to say what I mean, least of all to Ima. Carli is hot, of course she is, and she's fun to hang out with even if she does talk a lot. Yet somehow I know, without knowing why, that even if I did want to go out with her, I couldn't. Because of Becky. It's like Carli belongs to Becky and the rest of us need to stand back.

"It's just, do you know what's up with her and Becky? I'm not asking you to betray any secrets, I just... wondered." Ima watches my face for a reaction.

I look at her blankly. "What's up? Nothing's up. Except they seem to be glued together all the time. Becky's there now, isn't she?"

"No," says Ima thoughtfully. "She came home. I just

picked her up. Said she wasn't well, didn't want any tea. I don't know, perhaps I'm worrying about nothing."

"Well, there you go then. That's what's up. She's got a bug or something."

"Hmm. I invited her parents to the party." Her voice is casual, like when she's trying to make light of something serious.

"Oh, okay. Are they coming then?"

I don't really care. I wonder when Ima's going to go, so I can double-check those train times for when I go to meet Eli.

"No, I don't think so. Her mum was a bit funny about it actually. I'm not sure that they approve of us."

"What, cos they live in a big posh house in Cherry Avenue?"

"Yes, maybe it's that." But she doesn't sound sure.

"Ah well, their loss, more food for everyone else."

"You're always so sensible, Josh." She sighs. "Sometimes I feel like you're more grown up than me. But you know, if you need me, you can always talk to me. I know you won't believe me, but I do remember what it's like being a teenager. All those hormones…"

"Ima, stop. Stop now."

"Okay, I'm going, I'm going."

But when she finally does go, I can't settle. Maybe something *is* up with Becky. I'd better see if she's okay.

I knock on her bedroom door. Three quick taps followed by two slow ones. Our secret knock – the one we've had since we were little.

"Go away. I've gone to bed," comes a muffled voice from behind the door.

"What? Don't be stupid. It's only eight o'clock or something."

I shift from foot to foot outside the closed door. This isn't just me checking that she's all right. I really want to talk to her. I need her to tell me I'm doing the right thing. I take a deep breath.

"Come on, Becky, please, let me come in. There's something I need to ask you."

Silence. Except for a snuffling sound that could be nothing, just Becky moving something around in her room, or it could be the weather outside…or it could be crying.

"Becks," I ask, anxious, ear pressed against the door. "Are you okay?"

I wait for another minute. Nothing. Why won't she talk to me?

I raise my hand to knock again, and then let it fall. I walk away.

BECKY

"Hello, stranger."

I've been lying low all morning, trying to avoid Carli, trying to avoid everyone, but of course Archie's found me – huddled on one of the benches by the AstroTurf, staring into space. Last night's rain has cleared, but everything's still damp and there are grey clouds over our heads. Archie swings his bag off his shoulder, wipes some raindrops off the bench and settles down next to me. "Fancy seeing you here."

We sit in silence for a bit, but things are never quiet for long when Archie's around.

"Hello, Archie," he says. "How are you? Why yes, thank you, Archie, I'm fine… How was your evening, Archie? Oh, you know same as ever…"

I don't answer, just keep on staring at my feet. Eventually Archie breaks the silence.

"Come on, Becks, what's up? Tell me *all* about it."

"Not now, Archie, I'm not in the mood."

I still feel rotten after last night. Carli sent me messages all through the rest of the evening. Chirpy, hope-everything's-okay messages. Please-don't-ignore-me messages. Can-we-still-be-friends? messages. Fine-I'll-leave-you-alone-then messages. I haven't replied to any of them.

"Come on, Becks," Archie coaxes. "What's happened? You're not mad at me, are you? Why don't you want to talk to me?"

I should tell him. I can't tell him. What would happen if I did tell him? The words are almost there, but…

"You didn't tell me!" I snap suddenly.

Archie looks confused. "Didn't tell you what?"

"About Olivia. You didn't tell me that Olivia's bi."

"Whoa, what? Back up, you're in a mood with me because you think I knew Olivia was bi and I didn't tell you? Seriously?"

"Well?" I glare at him.

"You know, it's not like I've got some magic power where I can spot all the gays in the school." As he talks, Archie fiddles with the zip on his bag, pulling it up and

127

down, opening it and then shutting it again. It's driving me nuts. "And even if I did, do I then have to report them to you? Come on, Becky, don't be stupid."

"Olivia's not gay. She's bi," I snap back.

"Yeah, okay, I get that. But this isn't about Olivia. What's *really* up?"

"Archie?" I say sternly.

"Yeah, okay, I knew, but only since last week… It *is* pretty cool not being the only one who's out in Year Eight." He grins. "But really, Becks, so what? It's not like it's some big secret. Since when do you care about Olivia and what she does?"

"I care about you, not her." I'm not really angry at Archie, but my voice is getting louder so that I'm almost shouting at him now. Everything I say is coming out wrong, but I don't know how to make it right.

There was this nature programme I saw once, all about how different animals defend themselves when they feel under attack. Hedgehogs rolling up into prickly balls, or squid squirting out clouds of ink to confuse their enemies. There was this one tiny monkey, I can't remember what it was called, that just went wild, snapping and biting and making its hair stick out on end so it looked bigger, all before any predators got anywhere near it. Before even the slightest sign of an attack, it leaped into action, striking first so that no one could get near enough to threaten its safety.

My voice wobbles. "I care because you're my best friend. And that means you're supposed to tell me stuff, that's all."

"Oh really?" says Archie, taking a deep breath and then speaking all in a rush. "Well, Becks, I wasn't going to say this, but if I had *actually* seen you over the last few days, then maybe I *might* have told you about Olivia. But you seem to have been too distracted with your *new* best friend lately to even notice that I'm here. It's a bit much blaming me for not telling you something, when you've barely even said hello to me for days. Why don't you just ask Carli? I'm sure *she'd* be happy to help." His cheeks have gone bright red, which I know means he's upset but trying not to show it.

A cluster of Year Seven girls nearby break off their conversation and look curiously over at us to see what's going on. They can sense that something worth watching is happening.

"Oh, don't be such a drama queen!" I snap back.

"You know what, Becky, *I'm* not the one being the drama queen here. I just came to see if you were all right, but, you know what, I wish I hadn't bothered." He shoulders his bag and gets up. "See you around."

In my head, I'm running after him, I'm saying sorry and making everything okay again, and then we're laughing over how ridiculous we've both been and we're linking arms as we walk to French. But instead, I just sit here, frozen, as Archie sweeps off without even looking back.

I slowly gather up my things. The bell's about to go. The Year Sevens have already giggled and jostled their way off – show over – and the grounds are almost empty, but I want to put off going back inside for as long as I can. It's not like Archie and I haven't fought before. We've been friends for so long that we've fallen out and made up again more times than I can remember.

It will be okay, I tell myself, *everything will be okay. It always is.*

But I don't believe it.

As I turn the corner, back into the main building, someone else running the other way slams into me.

Books and pens scatter everywhere. Now, just to make things even worse, I *know* I'm going to be late and Mr Herbert will make some sarcastic comment in French that I don't understand and everyone will laugh. I bend down to help pick everything up, but it takes me a second to realize who is crouched down next to me.

"Sorry," says Carli. "I thought I was gonna be late, so I was running, and now I guess I'm *definitely* going to be late." She smiles at me tentatively. "I'm glad I saw you though. Thanks for helping. Sorry, I'm making you late too."

I keep my head down, picking up pens and handing them over to Carli without saying anything. Just hearing her voice again makes my stomach flip over. I want to look at her and I don't want to look both at the same time.

"You know," she says quietly, "I won't tell anyone about what happened, if that's what you're worried about. But, Becky, I can't—"

"There, that's everything," I interrupt. "I'd better go."

"Yeah, me too. See you at Pride group later?"

Ima's words from last night about not throwing friendship away flash back into my mind. That's exactly what I've been doing: throwing my friendships away. First Carli, then Archie. Even Josh – Josh and I always used to talk about everything, now I don't even know what's up with him. If I keep acting like this, there'll be no one left.

I look into her blue eyes. "Yeah, maybe." That's the best I can manage. I hope it's enough.

JOSH

I wouldn't admit it to Jayden or Max, but I've been looking forward to Pride group today. I'm not sure why. It's only the second meeting, but already it feels like we're becoming something more than just a collection of random people from different years.

I like it when Alex stops to say hi in the corridor, or yesterday when Kai and I were both running into school late and they flashed me a smile that said, *You too*. Maybe I like it just because everyone here's got something they're working through, so it makes my own stuff seem less weird.

Becky wouldn't talk to me last night. Maybe it's for the best. She might have tried to stop me meeting Eli or said that she'd tell Mum and Ima. Anyway, I can decide for myself. It's better that I check this out on my own first and then I can tell her all about Eli, once everything's certain in my mind.

This morning she left for school before I'd even started breakfast, but at least here I know I'll see her. Although, when I go through the rainbow-flag-covered door of the classroom and look around, she's not there. Odd, Becky's usually early.

"Is Becky coming?" Carli asks when she sees me come in.

I shrug. "Dunno, thought she'd be with you."

Carli looks down at her perfect nails. "I wasn't sure if she'd want to come – not now."

Before I can ask her what she's talking about, Olivia calls over to her. "Carli, these biscuits are so gorgeous. The icing's really cute as well."

There's more chatting and laughing and, just as things are settling down, Becky slips in next to me and looks around the room. Carli smiles at her, but Becky looks away. I feel her body tense next to mine.

"You're late," I mutter. "And what's up with you and Carli?"

"Nothing," she snaps. "And I'm here now, aren't I? But I'm not saying anything this week. No one can make me."

"That'll be a first then," I whisper back, and then quickly lean forward like I'm listening intently to what Alex is saying. Becky prods me in the back. I kick her under the table.

Becky sighs and shuffles next to me throughout the group. I wish she wasn't on such a downer today, not like last week when she was buzzing with ideas.

There are a few new people, so we do icebreakers again, but apart from that I just keep quiet and listen. There are enough people here with plenty to say that there's no silence to fill.

I let it all wash over me and go over the plans for Saturday in my head one more time. I'll set my alarm for 5.15. No one at home will be up *that* early. That gives me time to get up, grab my stuff, jump on my bike and get to the station for six. By the time Mum and Ima are up, I'll send a message, saying how I got up early and went to Jayden's, or for extra football training for the match next week. I'll think of something. I'll be in Manchester by nine – I can hang around in the station for a bit, no one will notice me there, and I'll still have ages before 11.30 to find out where McDonald's is and to be ready to meet Eli there.

The next part is harder to picture – the part where I

actually meet him. And when I do imagine it, it's more like a scene on TV than something which would happen in real life. Then I'll be back on the train at two, and home by five. Mum and Ima won't have a clue. Not till I choose to tell them anyway. So why do I feel sick just thinking about it? I've planned it out so carefully, why am I scared it will all go wrong?

It's ridiculous. I sound like Ima when she's going on and on about the surprise party: the time for this and the time for that, and who has to be where when. I swear she's got a schedule on an Excel sheet somewhere.

Suddenly everything freezes. I stop breathing, just for a second. In the far distance I can hear everyone talking excitedly about who's doing what for the assembly. Becky can tell something's wrong. She gives me a puzzled look, and I force myself to smile.

Saturday. *This* Saturday. The surprise party. What am I going to do?

BECKY

The sun's pouring through the curtains when I wake up. It feels like a good sign. Maybe it means that things are going to get better. After all, this week can't get any worse. Archie and I still haven't made up, and I think Carli's given up trying to talk to me because every time she does, I'm so horrible to her. Whenever I see her now she's surrounded by girls from the netball team. I ache with missing them both. I suppose I could hang out with some of the others from photography club instead, but I'm just not feeling in the mood to be with anyone. Instead I've been trying to keep out of everyone's way – even Mum and Ima and Josh – walking by the canal after school, just me and my camera, taking pictures of the boats and the birds and the light on the water.

But today is the party. Below me, stashed under my loft bed, are stacks of paper plates and bags of decorations, plus several boxes of wine glasses, each stamped with FRAGILE in red on the outside. Something new has appeared every day. Ima's been hiding them here during the week while Mum's been at work, ready for tonight.

I yawn and stretch, push my feet into my fluffy slippers and check the time – it's after nine already. Mum and Ima will soon be off to catch their train.

I can smell coffee from downstairs, which always makes me feel a bit sick in the mornings. When I get to the kitchen, the two of them are dressed and sitting at the table, sipping black coffee and eating croissants.

"Happy birthday, Mum!"

Mum beams at me. "Thanks, Becky. Here, give me a hug." So I lean into her. It's so comforting that I hold on a little bit longer than she's expecting.

"You know you're not getting your presents till you get back, don't you?" I say, as I finally pull away.

"I know I'm going to be spoiled rotten, I know that. Rushed straight from shul to a fancy lunch and then an afternoon out at a gallery. And then back home for a relaxing evening with my wife and my sister and my children – my favourite people. It's quite something. Maybe even worth being fifty for."

"Well," says Ima brightly, "it is a special day, isn't it?"

"Are you sure that you and Josh don't mind not coming today?" Mum looks worried.

Ima, standing behind her, makes frantic signs at me.

"No," I say firmly. "You should have your day out, just the two of you. We've got dinner here tonight to celebrate, haven't we? Anyway, we get to spend today with Auntie Jackie. We haven't seen her for ages."

"I'm so glad Jackie could come for the weekend," agrees Mum. "It's such a long way for her. Maybe I *should* be here when she arrives? We could wait, leave a bit later…" She looks thoughtful. "Hard to believe we're both in our fifties now. How on earth did that happen?"

"Fifty and still as beautiful as ever," says Ima, planting a kiss on the top of Mum's head.

"Ima, don't be gross," I say, squeezing behind her to get the milk out of the fridge. "Isn't Josh up yet?"

"What do you think?"

"He could have made an effort for your birthday," I grumble.

"It doesn't matter," says Mum. It seems like she's

always happy to give Josh some extra leeway. "We'll all be together tonight. I might just go and check on him though. Have we got time before we go, Ruth?"

"Of course," says Ima, and Mum heads upstairs.

As soon as she's out of the room, Ima turns to me.

"Are you all ready?" she whispers. "You've got the decorations, the presents, you know Neil's coming at five with the cake and the rest of the food—"

"Yes," I interrupt. "Yes, I know, I know. You've only told me about a million times. Once you've gone, I'll make sure Josh shifts out of bed, and we'll get started. Auntie Jackie'll be here soon anyway. Trust us. Okay?"

She puts her hands on my shoulders and looks me in the eyes. "Okay, all right."

"What are you two looking so secretive about?" asks Mum, popping her head round the kitchen door.

"Nothing!" Ima and I both say in unison, jumping apart, which makes us seem even more suspicious.

"Josh is out for the count," says Mum. "I knocked and then stuck my head in, but it's pitch-black in there and no sign of movement. I hope he's not coming down with something like you were earlier this week, Becky."

"Of course not," I say. "Stop worrying. Go and have fun!"

When they've finally gone, I settle down to my cornflakes.

Half an hour later, when I'm already fed up with what's on TV and there's still no movement from upstairs, I decide it's time to get Josh up.

I use our special knock. No reply. So I just thump on his door a couple of times. Nothing.

This is weird. Josh normally lies in whenever he gets the chance, but he knows how much we've got to do today before the party starts.

"Josh, get up you lazy lump. It's party time…"

I push open the door, flick the light on.

The bed's empty.

"Josh?" I call again, confused.

I step out of his room and check the bathroom, just in case he got up without me noticing. Not there.

Back in his room, I pull off the duvet and shake it out. Stupid. As if he could be hiding under there.

I'm not just confused now, I'm worried.

What's happened?

Where is Josh?

JOSH

I needn't have bothered setting the alarm after all. I was awake well before 5.15 a.m. I don't think I slept much all night, worrying that I'd lie in by mistake and miss my train, or that I'd get there and Eli wouldn't even show up.

I sneak out without disturbing anyone. The doors to Becky's room and Mum and Ima's are shut tight as I tiptoe past. I feel like a burglar, except that I am breaking out instead of in.

The click of the front door as I pull it shut sounds so loud that I pause for a moment on the step, heart thumping in my chest, straining for any sound of movement in the house. But it's all silent.

After that everything goes smoothly. Cycling's quick through the empty streets, and I manage to work the machines to buy the ticket, find the platform, and even have time to get the most enormous, sticky-sweet chocolate-filled pastry. The sort of pastry that Ima says is "a heart attack waiting to happen". I think about her and Mum, waking up and finding I'm not there, especially since it's not just an ordinary Saturday, it's Mum's birthday. I push the guilt away and tell myself that there'll be plenty of time to celebrate with her later. Anyway, no one will even have noticed I've gone. Yet.

It's quiet on the train too. In my carriage, there's only me and this old couple reading their newspapers at the next table. When I got on the train, they shot me such dirty looks, it was like I'd walked into their private sitting room. Now they keep sighing to themselves whenever I move. I guess they think I'm about to vandalize the train or start spraying graffiti on the windows.

I hope I never get like that when I'm old. I feel guilty enough already, without people who don't even know me making me feel like I've done something wrong. I pull my hood further down and stare out of the window, hoping they'll soon find something else to disapprove of and stop glaring at me.

I hope Becky doesn't mind too much. She's going to take a long time to forgive me for this. I hope she gets it when I explain. I'll be back before the party anyway, before the first guests even start arriving. What's the big deal? After all, I tried to tell her, didn't I? It's her fault that she didn't want to talk to me.

But it *is* a big deal, especially with the party tonight, I know that really, and the worst of it is going behind her back.

Crewe. Wilmslow. Stockport. At each station, the carriage fills up. Streets and houses replace the fields. People get on and get off, laughing and chatting, but the old couple are still here, sipping from their flasks and unwrapping their sandwiches. Then, finally, we arrive.

Manchester Piccadilly station is huge. So much bigger than Watford Junction. The lights are so bright and people are dashing everywhere. Everyone seems to know where they are going. Except me. I catch a glimpse of my reflection in the train window. I look transparent, like I'm not even really there. I don't even look thirteen, let alone the age I've told Eli I am – I look like a lost child.

I pull back my shoulders and try to look taller. I even smile at my image in the glass, trying to make myself look and feel braver. I find a place to sit and wait, a cold metal seat by one of the platforms. I watch friends hug each other, hear people shriek as they spot the person they're waiting for come off the train, see little kids running away and being brought back again by their parents. Everyone is with someone. Except me. No one even knows I'm here.

My phone buzzes, angrily, insistently.

Oh no, I never sent the message to Ima and Mum about my made-up football training. I was so focused on getting here that I totally forgot. I bet it's them.

But it's not Ima or Mum. It's Becky.

Where ru?

I take a few minutes before messaging her back. I can't lie to Becky, not outright. She'd never believe me anyway. This would be the time to 'fess up, wouldn't it?

All ok. Had to do something important, PLS tell auntie Jackie I'm ok but DON'T let her tell Ima. Thx. Back soon.

I hesitate again, before adding Sorry.

I don't reply to the messages from Becky that follow. I scroll through the ones from Eli instead, double-checking that it's the right day.

There are lots of messages from the last week. At first I asked him about his mum and what it was like being interviewed for the magazine (part embarrassing, part cool, apparently), but since then we haven't really talked about why we joined the forum or even really about being donor-conceived (I'm getting used to calling it "DC" now). Which is weird, cos that's the thing we've got in common. Without that, we wouldn't even know each other, we'd have no reason to meet.

I've got so many questions for him. But I haven't asked them yet. I don't want to ask about the donor or tell him that I think he's my brother, not until I meet him. It just doesn't feel right in a message. I don't think I'll be able to find the right words until I meet him face to face. He doesn't ask many questions either, which is good because I don't want to say anything that might make him think I'm younger than I say I am, or that would make him change his mind and say that he doesn't want to meet me after all.

Instead we've just been messaging about everyday stuff, like school or football or TV, plus he usually has some stupid story that makes me laugh about his dog, Maggie, who's always getting into trouble. But mostly it's just saying hi, how are you? Every time I get a notification now, I wonder, is it him? We haven't met yet, but I already feel like I know him.

I keep thinking about what it will be like to actually meet him. I'm excited but nervous too. I wonder how he'd feel about having a brother. What will he say when I tell him that I think we've got the same donor, that I think we're related? Maybe he'll even think the same thing once he meets me, maybe he's already been wondering since I got in touch. He's an only child, I know that from his messages. He's probably always wanted a brother.

"Anyone sitting here, love?"

I move my bag off the seat next to mine, and a smiley woman with loads of luggage settles herself down. She's a bit older than Mum and Ima, more like Auntie Jackie's age, except not nearly as smartly dressed. I feel another stab of guilt – Auntie Jackie will be arriving at our house about now and wondering where I am. This is all so much more complicated than I thought it would be. It's obvious now, but I hadn't really thought about Becky or Auntie Jackie and how me disappearing could make trouble for them. I just want to meet Eli, that's all, that's the only reason why I'm here. I didn't want to mess things up for anyone else. But there's nothing I can do right now to make things better for them, so I try not to think about it.

The woman arranges her bags around her feet and pulls out a packet of biscuits. She takes one and bites into it with enthusiasm. Seeing me watching her, she turns to me.

"Aye, I know, not very healthy, is it? I'm just having the one though. A bit of sweetness with my coffee. Would you like one? I can't sit here eating these by myself, can I now?"

I hesitate.

"Ah, go on, you look like you need feeding up."

"Thank you." I take a biscuit, but I hope this doesn't mean she's going to spend all morning talking to me.

"It's a good place to stop here, you can see the board really well, shame about all those blessed delays, always the same," she continues. "Which train are you waiting for then?"

"I'm not waiting for a train," I say. "I'm meeting someone and I got here a bit early."

She looks at me closely. "I see. I thought you looked a bit young to be travelling by yourself. But then, kids grow up so fast these days." She helps herself to another biscuit and waves the packet at me again.

I'm not sure what to say to this, but she has so much to say that I don't need to reply, so I just take another biscuit.

"I'm waiting for the Edinburgh train – if it ever comes. I'm off to see my sister, just to spend a few days with her and with my nieces. They're a bit older than you, I reckon, proper young ladies."

"I'm meeting up with my big brother," I say. It's the first time I've tried these words out, the first time I've spoken them to someone else. It feels weird but good. Definitely good. Makes it feel more real. "He works near here."

"Oh, that's nice. Are you two close then? Me and my sister, we've always been close. Even though we live a way apart now, that doesn't really make any difference. Say what you like, there's nothing more important than family."

"Well, I guess we're pretty close." She's not to know I've never met him before. "Yeah, we hang out a lot together actually."

"Oh look, there's my platform at last." She heaves herself to her feet and gathers up all her bags. "Here, you take the rest of these, go on, you can share them with your brother. I'd only eat them all and that's not good for me." She chuckles to herself. "I hope you two boys have a lovely day together."

Before I've had a chance to say thank you, she's shuffled away. I shove the biscuits in my bag. Her words echo in my mind: *there's nothing more important than family.*

BECKY

"I wouldn't worry," says Auntie Jackie, propping her little wheelie suitcase in the corner of my room and getting out her make-up bag. "I'm sure he'll be back soon. Maybe he's just getting some last-minute bits for the party."

"There *are* no last-minute bits. Ima and I have got everything. It's all here. There's nothing he needs to get. He always thought this party was a bad idea, and now he's just disappeared…" My voice is getting higher and higher.

She puts her hand on my arm to stop me talking. "Becky, you know Josh, he's pretty reliable, right?" I nod reluctantly. She's right; Josh *is* reliable. Reliable going on boring, sometimes. That's why this is so odd. "He'll be

150

back before we know it. Now, we've got a lot to do and a very special party to put on."

She frowns briefly. "I am looking forward to seeing him though. I'm not here for long this time. I hope he's back soon, so I can make the most of seeing you both. But first things first, I need a coffee and you need to take me through the plans."

"I still think it's weird," I grumble. "Like you say, it's not like Josh. He should be here."

She finishes doing her lipstick and snaps the lid back on. "If you're worried, why don't you call him? He'll have his phone, won't he?"

"I've messaged him. He just said he was doing something important and would be back soon, so…"

"So he will. I'm sure he won't be that long."

"Okay," I say reluctantly.

"Now – coffee."

Jackie drinks her coffee while I upend the box of photos and spread the contents across the kitchen table.

"So the idea is, we string these up along the living-room walls and the stairs. I've got some ribbon and these little silver clips. It's like a photo gallery of Mum's life. I'm the curator."

151

"This is such a good collection. How did you get all these?"

"Well, some of Mum's friends sent us them or emailed them, then Ima found all the old albums in the loft and saved them when Mum was threatening a clear-out, then there are the ones I've taken."

"And you've done all this without your mum suspecting anything? That's pretty amazing, Becky. She is going to be so surprised – and proud of you."

I start to sort through the photos in front of me. "I don't think we should try to do them in order, that's too hard. Do you think we should try or just mix them all up?"

"Mixing them up sounds good to me, but I'm just the assistant, remember, not the curator. I'm here to take orders about what's to be done. There's a bit of a gap though, isn't there? From when she was younger?"

"Yeah, I know…"

"Good job I remembered to bring this then."

She produces an envelope from her bag with a flourish and tips the contents onto the table. Out spill photos – baby photos, photos of chubby-faced little girls in party dresses, faded photos of gawky teenagers with bad haircuts and so many more. "You won't want *all* these, of course, but once I started collecting them together, I just couldn't stop."

"Oh wow, these are brilliant. I'm definitely going to need all of this ribbon now. Let's put up as many as we can. Is this really you and Mum?" I point to a picture of a beaming little girl, balancing a bundle of baby wrapped in white wool blankets on her lap.

"Yes, that's really us. Oh, I was so excited to have a little sister. I thought it was the best present ever. Not that we didn't fight, and she wound me up something rotten, but she was always my sister. We were always a team of two. Well, you know how it is, just like you and Josh."

I twist the ribbon between my fingers. "Did you tell each other everything?" I ask.

"No, not everything," Jackie says thoughtfully. "I always kept my diary hidden from her and from our mum and dad – your grandma and grandpa. I bet you do the same with yours, don't you?"

I nod.

"But I suppose we did tell each other all the important stuff. Except sometimes we knew anyway without being told, if you see what I mean. She's the person who knows me best in the world. How many other people have I known for half a century, eh?"

"What about…" I pause, keeping my eyes fixed on the photos on the table. I've been wondering about this all week. "What about when she told you she was gay? What was that like?"

Auntie Jackie gets up and walks over to the sink. She turns on the tap and starts slowly rinsing out her cup. It's like she knows it's easier for me to talk when we're not sitting at the table, staring at each other.

"I can't believe I haven't told you about this. Your mum was away, doing her nursing degree. She worked so hard, much harder than I'd done at university. It was the end of her second year and she was coming home for Christmas. I'd just passed my driving test, so I went to pick her up from the station. She told me on the way home. All about this girl she'd met…"

"Was that Ima?" I ask.

"No, she didn't meet Ruth till much later. It was…oh god, I forget her name now. Isn't that awful? It's so long ago. I do remember how nervous she was about telling me, but also how happy she looked."

"Why was she nervous? What did she think you'd say?"

"I'm not sure. It sounds odd now, but we just didn't know many gay people back then. No one really talked

154

about it. I know I sound really old saying it, but people just weren't as accepting as they are now. Not by a long way. I think she would have been nervous telling anyone, let alone the people who mattered most to her."

She turns to face me again, smiling, leaning back against the kitchen counter. "Anyway, I haven't told you what happened next. I was so surprised that my beautiful little sister – who'd always had boyfriends and loved doing girly stuff – was gay, and I was still so new to driving, that I forgot what I was doing, turned round to look at her and drove straight into a parked car."

My hand shoots up to my mouth in surprise. It's hard to imagine anyone as calm and smart and in control as Auntie Jackie crashing her car.

"No one was hurt, thankfully, but it made this awfully loud crunch. Like an explosion. I was just so embarrassed. I'd only been driving for a month!" She shakes her head, like all these years later, she still can't believe it really happened.

I glance at the time on my phone. We should be starting the decorations by now, but there's something else I want to know.

"Were you glad she'd told you? I mean, despite the accident and everything."

"Yes," says Auntie Jackie firmly. "I wish she'd picked a better time, but yes. It's always better to be honest than to keep secrets. Most of all for the person with the secret. Nothing she could have told me would have made me love her any less."

I look up, and she meets my eyes. This time, I know I shouldn't look away.

"Becky, are you okay?" she says. "You know if there's anything you want to talk to me about, anything at all, that I'll listen. The same's true for you as for your mum. Nothing you could say will make me love you less. Nothing."

Auntie Jackie sits down next to me and waits. She's so calm and still.

My throat's gone dry. "It's just…" I start. "It's just there's this girl…"

And it all comes spilling out. She doesn't interrupt. She doesn't even move, apart from quietly handing me a tissue from her handbag when I need it.

"I just don't know why I'm upset," I finish. "It's just me making a big deal out of nothing, isn't it?"

She doesn't rush to answer. "I wouldn't say that, not at all. Having someone you really like turn you down isn't nothing. It's one of the worst things there is. It hurts so much," she says gently. "And when it also means that you've discovered something about yourself that you didn't know before, that's even more difficult. It's okay to feel like this."

I blow my nose loudly. Great look for a party – all red-eyed and sniffing.

"But some people might say," continues Auntie Jackie carefully, "that having parents like yours would be an advantage. That they'd be the first people you could go to, because they'd understand where you were coming from."

I shake my head fiercely, shredding the tissue in my hands.

"So you haven't told them any of this?"

"No, not yet. You won't say anything, will you?"

Auntie Jackie looks at me. "Not if you don't want me to. But do you think you should? It might make you feel better."

"I don't want them to think…I don't know, that I'm copying them or just saying it because of them. It's nothing to do with them. I think they've always just assumed me and Josh would both be straight, like everyone else. Anyway, what if I tell them and I'm wrong and this is just a phase…"

But I know as soon as I say the words that this doesn't feel like a phase. If it wasn't Carli, it would have been some other girl, some other time. Now that I know that, imagining having a boyfriend or falling in love with a guy one day feels totally bizarre. It's like that famous photo – the one with a shark sticking out of the roof of someone's ordinary house in Oxford. The shark makes sense, and the house makes sense, but the two of them together make no sense at all.

"It's up to you. No one has to come out as straight after all, do they? It's up to you to find the right time. But maybe not when they're driving, okay? For everyone's safety!" She laughs, and that makes me smile a watery smile too.

After a few seconds, she's serious again, her voice so quiet that I lean in to hear her. "But don't leave it too long. They love you so much, you and Josh, the babies they thought they'd never have. It wouldn't change a thing, but I think they'd still want to know."

We sit in silence for a moment. There's nothing more that needs to be said. She reaches out to squeeze my hand, and suddenly we both jump as there's a loud knock on the front door.

JOSH

I see him before he sees me.

I'd got there ten minutes before we'd arranged to meet, bought a Coke and found a table in the corner with a good view of the door. Just after 11.30 a.m., I see a tall guy with dark hair come in. I watch him while he looks around, as if searching for a familiar face. He's taller than I expected, but same face, same hair, same smile.

I take a deep breath – this is it – and raise my hand to wave to him.

He smiles and comes over. "You're Josh?"

"Yes, that's me." My voice sounds high and tight, like I'm just a kid, but Eli doesn't seem to notice. I clear my throat.

He puts out his hand to shake. "Eli. I've only got an

hour for lunch, but I reckon we've still got plenty of time to talk. It's great you live so near."

I nod. It doesn't feel so much like lying if I don't say the actual words.

"Cool, well, I'll just get some chips. You want anything?"

As he queues, I think to myself, *Here I am, just hanging out with my brother. Nothing could be more ordinary.* On the table, my phone buzzes again. My bag's on the chair next to me, so I shove my phone underneath, well out of the way. I don't want anything to disturb us.

"Normally I get a free lunch at work, before the rush starts. It feels well weird to be eating someone else's chips," says Eli, putting down his tray on the table, ripping open the bag of chips and pushing it towards me so that I can help myself. I take a chip, but my mouth's too dry to taste anything. "But I thought here would be better to talk. People at work don't know I'm DC. They are nosy though. They probably think I'm meeting some girl!"

"So you work at Nando's, right?"

"Yeah, the one just round the corner. You know it? No, never mind. It's just like every other Nando's. It's okay, just for Saturdays and the odd Sunday. Anyway, you wanted to talk…"

This is the bit I've planned. "Yeah, I just wanted to meet someone else who's donor-conceived…I mean DC." It feels strange being able to say "DC" out loud to someone who knows what it means. I stumble over it at first. "Apart from my sister. On the forum you seemed, I don't know, really sorted about it all. You're the first person I've actually met who knows what it's like."

Eli nods. "So when did you find out?" he asks through a mouthful of chips.

"When I was little. I don't remember not knowing. We even had this book explaining it all…"

"*Our Story*? Yeah, I had *Our Story* too. I used to love that book. You're like me then, not one of these angry DC kids?"

"Angry?"

"Yeah, you know, like the ones in the group who found out by mistake or whose parents kept it a secret. Some even say they wish they'd never been born cos of how unfair it is not knowing where they come from. Always going on about how miserable they are, how selfish their parents are."

"Yeah, I read some of those posts too. But not wanting to have been born, I don't get it, that's pretty extreme."

"I know, that's not how I feel. My mum wanted a kid,

she didn't meet the right man, so she just got on with it. That's fair enough. And she was always honest about it, so that's fine with me. I'm like her, always really logical about everything."

Another thing we've got in common. I wonder what else. "Your mum – is she Jewish?" I ask.

"Jewish? No, why?"

"Just wondered. My family's Jewish. Elijah's kind of a Jewish name."

He laughs. "You know why I'm called Elijah? It's cos my mum is a huge fan of the *Lord of the Rings* films. The ones with Elijah Wood. That's why she named me Elijah, after him. Everyone calls me Eli though."

"At least she didn't name you 'Bilbo Baggins'."

He smiles. I feel good that he liked my joke, even though he must have heard it hundreds of times before.

"God, that would have been a nightmare. Although I guess I could have been just 'Bill' instead. That I definitely would have kept secret. Anyway, what about your mum? Is she okay about you being in the forum, talking to other DC kids?"

"A bit… Well, not really." I take a deep breath. "Actually, my parents don't know about that. I mean, not yet. I'm going to tell them soon."

"You've got to do it your way," says Eli, leaning back in his chair. "It's your life, not theirs. Not everyone's as into it as my mum. She's more into the DC stuff than I am, to be honest. Well, you saw that article!" He raises his eyebrows. "Some parents can be really funny about kids looking for their donors, even talking about them. Especially the dads – they see it as a threat or something. That's what my mum says anyway."

"I haven't got a dad – apart from the donor, I mean. I've got two mums. They wanted kids, and one of my mums tried for ages at a clinic but didn't get pregnant. Then my other mum tried at the same clinic, and *she* got pregnant first time. But then my mum found out she was pregnant too. Same donor for both of us though. So they were both pregnant at the same time in the end. Me and Becky, she's my sister, we were born only eight days apart."

Eli pauses eating and looks up.

"So she's your sister, but you've got different mums?"

"Yeah, biologically we have. And, like I said, same donor, so we're still blood-related. But, you know, it's not like my biological mum is more my mum than my other mum is. Does that make any sense?"

"Sure." He nods, taking another handful of chips.

"You're sure you don't want any more?" I shake my head. "Okay, but genes or whatever must matter to you. Otherwise you wouldn't be here, would you? You wouldn't be in the forum or asking questions about being a DC kid. You wouldn't be here with me – you'd be playing football or watching TV or lying in on a Saturday morning."

I'm not ready to tell him that I think he's my brother, not yet, so I turn the question back.

"Why did you agree to meet me?" I ask.

He sighs. "Because it's confusing, isn't it? And people don't really understand, even if they say they do. They still ask if you miss your dad, or if you're good at stuff because of him, or why your mum used a donor when she could have adopted a child instead. It's annoying. I hate it. I can talk about it with my mum, and even though she's really keen for me to find my donor one day and meet siblings when I'm ready, I don't want to make her feel bad by asking too much. I used to spend ages reading posts online, but sometimes it's not enough, you need someone right there who gets it. So, I thought, if you needed to talk, I know what that feels like, so okay."

"Thanks." I smile. "Really. I worried you'd think I was making too big a deal out of this. That's what Becky thinks. She says it doesn't matter who our donor is, that he's got nothing to do with us."

I've never talked about this with anyone before, except Becky, who wasn't interested in finding the donor, and she didn't know any more than I did. This is totally different. Everything Eli says opens up new thoughts and ideas and questions.

"So you haven't met your dad…I mean, your donor?" I ask.

He shakes his head. "When I got to sixteen, Mum and I did that thing where you can apply for 'non-identifying information', but we didn't find out much. You done that yet? No, well, it was a bit useless really, I don't think it's worth it. I'll just wait till I'm eighteen and see if I want to get in touch with him then."

My heart sinks. So Eli *isn't* going to be able to help me find my dad – *our* dad – at least not yet. But at least I've met him now. "But how *can* you wait?"

He shrugs. "People do all sorts of stuff to try and find out – DNA tests, ancestry websites, sharing their donor numbers online. I guess I'm not that desperate. Eighteen's not that long to wait."

Maybe not for him, but it is for me.

He leans forward and lowers his voice. "Don't get me

wrong, I want to know. I want to understand half of who I am. I want to meet him and see what he's like and find out how much he's like me. I want him to look at me and think, *Yeah, I'm glad I did that all those years ago*. I want him to be proud of me."

I'm nodding vigorously. That's exactly it. "That's just what I want too, so why—"

He holds up his hand to stop my question and keeps going. "But I know it might not happen how I want it to. I want him to be ready for me to find him, as well as me being ready to meet him."

All the time we're talking, I wonder how he can't see it. How can't he see that we look the same, sound the same, that he's my brother? He *must* be. Mustn't he? I feel more sure now that I've met him than I did before. At the very least, there's got to be a good chance.

But if he *has* seen the similarities, why doesn't he say anything? There are only a couple of minutes till he's got to go. I can't have come all this way, risked making Becky and Ima and Mum mad, and spent all this money, without taking this chance.

He's gathering together his stuff, checking his phone, ready to move. I don't want him to leave, so I blurt out another question. "So, er, what about siblings? I read an article about this one girl who found out she had brothers and sisters all over the world and went round meeting them all – that would be pretty amazing, right?"

"Sure, I'm interested in finding siblings out there, one day maybe…"

"It's just that…" My voice has gone faint again. I cough to clear my throat. "What if you were to meet a sibling right now, today?"

His eyes change as I'm speaking…from open and relaxed to guarded, suspicious.

"What?" he says, confused. "What are you talking about?"

This doesn't feel right, but I keep going. Once he knows, then it will all be okay. I try to swallow. My throat feels so dry that it's hard to get the words out, even though saying these words is the whole reason I'm here.

"It's me. I mean, think…I'm your brother."

There's a silence that seems to go on and on and on.

"Hey, what? Come on, don't wind me up, Josh." His voice is loud and irritated now. A couple of people at the next table look over. He notices them staring, and then lowers his voice again. "I didn't think you were one of those crazies. Look, it's been good to meet you, but I need to get back to work." He picks up his bag and stands.

"I mean it, it's true. At least, I think... I..."

But he's already walking away. I grab my stuff quickly and walk alongside him as he weaves his way through the tables towards the doors. I keep having to increase my pace as he speeds up, apologizing to the people that I push past in my hurry. He doesn't even look back at me.

Finally, when we're on the street, he turns to me. "So, what? You've had a DNA test?" I shake my head. "You've matched up my donor number and yours?" I shake my head again. "So how *do* you know?"

"I just know. You know how you said that you always approach everything logically, just like your mum does? Well, I'm like that too. I'm just the same. I saw your picture online and I just knew."

"You just knew?" he echoes. "Listen to yourself. That doesn't sound very logical."

"No, what I mean is, when I saw your picture I knew, because we look the same. Your eyes. Your face. It's obvious. You *must* see it." I can't let this go now. I can't.

"Look..." His voice is softer now, his eyes pitying. This is worse. "I can see why you want to think this. I know how appealing the idea of finding someone is. I feel it too. Always wondering, when I see someone in the street who looks familiar, is that person connected to me? But you and me – okay, we've both got dark hair, so what? I'm not your brother, Josh. I'm just someone you met on the internet. I should have known when I first saw you. I should have known this was weird. It was obvious straight away you're not sixteen like you said you were. How old are you? Thirteen? Fourteen?"

"Thirteen," I whisper. I can't meet his eyes any more.

"Thirteen." He shakes his head. "And your parents don't know about any of this? Jesus. You should have told me the truth."

"I thought you might not want to meet me if you thought I was that young. I thought I'd miss my chance."

"Listen, Josh, you didn't need to lie, I was happy to meet, to talk, I wanted to help you out, but you can't lay this on me, okay? Go home. If you want to know who you are, go talk to your parents, not me, not someone you just met. I'm sorry."

I watch him walk off and, within seconds, he's disappeared among the crowds. I could follow him. I know where he works. I could go there and find him and refuse to leave.

But I don't. I feel like all my energy has drained away. Like I've run a marathon but can't make it to the finish line. Eli's right – I shouldn't have done this. All I want to do now is go home.

I trudge back up the hill in a daze. I jump when someone shouts at me to get out of the way of the tram, but apart from that, I keep my eyes on my feet. The crowds grow even thicker as I get nearer to the station. I almost have to push my way onto the concourse.

During my long wait this morning, I'd already worked out which platform I'd need for my train home, so I know which way to go, but no one's moving anywhere. Instead, everyone's standing, looking up at the departure boards. There are people in red uniforms and reflective jackets scattered throughout the crowd, each with a cluster of passengers gathered round them who are asking questions or waving their hands around. I look up at the board.

Instead of a list of times, next to every destination is just one word, in bright orange capitals: DELAYED, DELAYED, DELAYED…

BECKY

There's a second knock, louder this time.

"Are you expecting a delivery?" asks Auntie Jackie. "Or an early guest?"

"No." I shake my head, confused. "Neil's coming first with the food, but that's not for ages yet, and everything else is here. I can't think of anyone who's supposed to arrive before lunch."

"Well then, maybe it's Josh, perhaps he's forgotten his key," she says, trying to sound reassuring. "I'll get it, you go and freshen up a bit."

I hope she's right. If it *is* Josh, then I won't have to worry about him any more. Then maybe this bad feeling in my stomach will go away.

I always kind of know when Josh is in trouble. Don't

ask me how. Like that time last year when he fractured his wrist at football practice. All evening, I had the same bad feeling I've got now – I knew something had happened, I just didn't know what it was, not until Josh was back home, cradling his arm and wincing and pretending to Mum and Ima that it was nothing.

I look at myself in the bathroom mirror. Staring back is a girl with wild hair, swollen eyes, a blotchy face and red nose. What would anyone – girl or boy – see in me anyway? I look a mess. I bite my lip to stop myself crying again, to stop myself replaying in my mind for the thousandth time what happened with Carli on Tuesday. Only after splashing cold water on my face and running it over my wrists do I start to feel better. But I can't stay in the bathroom all day, however rotten I feel. I'm ready to face Josh now and to get him to tell me what he's really been up to this morning.

I wonder how Ima and Mum are getting on in London. They're probably at the gallery by now. I hope Mum's having the most amazing day. I want tonight to be so special too, not just for her, but for Ima as well. I can't rely on Josh, not after he's already messed us about this morning. It feels like so much more depends on me now.

When I come out of the bathroom, it's not Josh, it's Archie.

He and Auntie Jackie are standing in the kitchen with their backs to the door, chatting easily together. She's pretending to be amazed by how tall he's got since she last saw him and he's gushing over her scarf. Whenever she comes to stay, Archie's usually around too. He's the only one of my friends that she knows really well.

"Archie's come to help set up for the party – isn't that great?" says Jackie, turning when she hears me come in.

Her face clouds over. "Archie, do *you* know where Josh is?" Casual, but with an undertone of worry.

"Sorry, no," says Archie. "Isn't he here?"

Jackie and I shake our heads.

"Well, thank goodness I came! You'll need the extra help," exclaims Archie.

"I think we'd have managed," I find myself saying. "Josh wouldn't have been much use anyway."

We all stand in awkward silence.

"Right, well… Tell you what, why don't you two start on the garden? I'll just hoover quickly inside. Where do your mums keep all the cleaning stuff, Becky?"

"Under the stairs," I reply.

"Okay then." And she's gone, leaving Archie and me

alone in the kitchen. He's holding an enormous bunch of flowers.

"Oh, those are gorgeous, Archie, they must have cost loads. What are they for?"

"I saw them and I thought, *those* would be just perfect to match my outfit. And the florist, who by the way was super cute, threw together this little bouquet just for me, and well – here they are!"

I stare at him for a moment.

"Becky, you idiot. They're for the party, and to say happy birthday to your mum, and they're also to kind of say sorry-and-can-we-be-friends-again? to you. Got it now?"

This is how it always goes when Archie and I fight. He's always the one to crack first and say sorry, whichever one of us started it. Somehow, he always knows exactly when I'm ready to stop being stubborn or sulky and need him to come and help me find a way back to being normal again. I feel a huge wave of relief sweep over me. At least one thing is going to turn out all right.

"No, no, stop, don't hug me now. Let me put the flowers down first," he protests, holding the bunch far above his head where I can't reach them. I ignore his squeals and grab him round the waist in a huge hug.

"Stop it, you'll squash them, you'll squash me," he carries on complaining, but it's only for effect, he's laughing too.

In the garden, Archie stands on a chair, stringing lights between the trees and along the fence. I'm on the ground, directing, urging him to move them higher or lower, until they're perfect. We drape rainbow bunting between the branches, tangling ourselves up in the process, and scatter picnic rugs and garden chairs on the grass. I take photos of how the garden looks now, knowing that by the time Mum and Ima see it, it will be full of people and noise, and there will probably already be dirty plates and half-empty glasses everywhere. But now, it looks magical. Like time has paused, waiting just for them.

Archie has helped make it look so much better, I must admit, than if it had just been me and Josh.

Auntie Jackie has finished the hoovering and started making the punch. We're not allowed the real thing, the alcoholic version, but she mixes up juices and flavours it with mint just for us and brings us each out a glass with ice to try, along with a sandwich. It must be well past lunchtime already, but we've been too busy to notice.

It's hot outside and the sky above the garden is a deep shade of blue, a perfect late-spring day.

Archie and I are lying on one of the rugs, his head on my lap. Even though I know there's still so much to do, I feel totally relaxed, like I could drift off to sleep.

"So, Beckster," Archie says lazily, his eyes closing. "What *was* that all about?"

I pause for a moment – should I tell him about what happened with Carli? Auntie Jackie was so brilliant. But what if Archie says the wrong things and makes me feel worse again?

Come on, though, this is Archie. I'll have to tell him sooner or later. And he's always on my side. Thinking about it, he's the perfect person to tell. I can't even really remember why we fought anyway.

"Oh," I say. "You won't believe this. Promise you won't scream when I tell you. I, well, I kissed Carli."

His eyes snap open again. "You did what? You kissed her? Oh my god. What happened? Becky, I can't believe you held out on me. Don't I always tell you everything? What was it like?"

"I didn't think about it, it just happened." I sigh. "But she didn't kiss me back, and then it was awful. So embarrassing." Saying it out loud, like it's a story that happened to someone else, takes some of the awfulness away, but just thinking about it still makes me wince. I have to stop myself from hiding my face in my hands.

He sits up and faces me. Serious, intense. "So does this mean you're gay? It does! You're gay and I didn't even know. *I'm* the one who should be mad at you, Becky. I should be storming off in a huff, but you're lucky, I'm too gossip-hungry to leave now. Oh my god, this is brilliant, I want to know everything. I'm bursting with questions."

"Me too. I've been looking at people all week – do I fancy him? Do I fancy her? Is she cuter than him? I don't know. It doesn't seem to work like that for me. I don't fancy *anyone*. Well, except Carli, that is. And that's a total disaster."

"So *that's* why you two haven't been speaking," he says thoughtfully. "Was she awful? What's she doing turning up to Pride group and everything, all full of smiles, after what she did to you? Poor Becks."

"No, no, it wasn't like that at all. She was really nice, honestly. That almost made it worse. She's said she still wants to be friends…" Archie makes a face. "I know, but in a nice way. But I just can't. Every time I see her, I feel bad and then I'm horrible to her which only makes me feel worse, but I can't stop wanting to see her. It's like having a bruise and wanting to poke at it all the time to see if it still hurts. Except she's not like a bruise…"

He leans his head on my shoulder. It's not the most comfortable position, as he's so much taller than me, but it feels good to be so close to someone.

"How could I not know? How rubbish must my gaydar be if I couldn't even spot you right next to me!"

"Not everything's about you! And seeing as I didn't even know myself, I feel pretty stupid too – like, my best friend's gay, my mums are gay. It's not like years ago when no one talked about it. It shouldn't exactly be a shock…"

"But it is, right?" he says gently.

"Yeah, it is. I'm just not ready to go telling everyone, to make a big deal out of it. Why's it anyone else's business? Maybe I'm just not going to be into the whole labels thing."

"That's a cop-out!"

"What?"

"A cop-out. Look, if someone else puts a label on you and uses that to define you or put you in a box or to treat you like dirt, then of course that's bad. But when people say that they're not into labels, it's probably because they've bought the whole idea that being LGBTQ or whatever is bad, so they don't want to be associated with it. But labels can be good if you reclaim them, then you can share who you are with other people and be stronger together."

"Very profound." I sound sarcastic but actually I'm impressed, even if I don't want Archie to know it.

Archie grins. "Actually, your mum told me that. She's right though."

I snort, as if to say, *Believe that if you like.* "You make being gay sound like being part of some kind of exclusive club."

"That's because it is, babes, it is. Oh, this is so exciting! I can't believe you sat through those Pride group meetings and didn't say a thing. So have you told your mums? What about Josh? You're so lucky with your family. Not like me."

He lapses into silence. I know what he's thinking about.

Archie wanted Mum to go with him when he came out to his own mum. She wouldn't, said it was something he had to do by himself, and anyway that it would be better if she wasn't there, as his mum might think she'd put him up to it or something. But she also said that she was just a text away if he needed her and he could come round here straight after if he wanted to talk.

Archie didn't tell me every gory detail about what happened – just that there was a lot of shouting and, since then, nothing. It's like the conversation never happened. I'm grateful that Ima and Mum won't be like that. Every holiday, when he goes up to stay with his dad, Archie says he's going to tell him, but I think he's still too nervous to actually do it.

"Well, I don't know if I want to tell them. Not yet." I pull up a couple of blades of grass and start plaiting them together.

"What? Seriously? Why not? They'll be so cool with it. In fact, I bet they'll be delighted. Throw you a party or something. I know…" He grasps my hand. "You should tell them tonight. It would be perfect, another birthday surprise for your mum."

I'm about to tell him the story about how Mum came out to Auntie Jackie, and why surprises aren't always such a good idea, when Jackie appears through the open French windows.

"It's looking great out here," she says, stepping outside from the shadows into the warmth. "And you both look so relaxed, but I'm sorry, I need your help to make it just as gorgeous inside. It's not that long till Neil will be getting here with the food." We get to our feet slowly, reluctant to move out of the sun and back into the dimness of the house. "Oh, and what's the plan for music for this party? I thought we could put it on now. Get ourselves in the mood."

"Music? That's Josh. He was doing a playlist." I check the time – it's later than I thought. The worried feeling in my stomach, which I've been trying to ignore all day, is still there. "Where *is* he?"

"Still no messages since this morning?" asks Jackie. "That's odd." She's starting to look more worried now.

"I'll message him again," I say. "And I'll go see what I can find in his room. I'm sure I can get the playlist off his tablet." I sound more relaxed than I feel. "Honestly, he's in *such* trouble when he gets back. Come on, Archie."

Josh's room is spotless as usual, barely a thing out of place, apart from the crumpled ball of duvet that I left on the floor from when I went in this morning. His tablet's on his desk and it only takes me a couple of guesses to get the passcode. While I'm looking, Archie runs his fingers along the top of Josh's books on the shelves.

"Wow, did you know he even has his books in height order? Is your brother for real? Perhaps he's not really a teenager at all, but a librarian disguised in a teenager's body?"

It's easy to find the playlist I'm after. Then I notice there's a message window open. It's not that I want to pry into Josh's secrets, but...I start reading, casually at first and then with increasing urgency.

"Oh my god," exclaims Archie, peeking in the wardrobe. "I think even his clothes are colour-coded."

"Archie," I say urgently, still looking at the screen. "Come and look at this. Now."

He leans over my shoulder as I point at the screen.

"These messages. They're all with this one guy, Eli." I turn round to look at Archie. "Do *you* know an Eli?"

"Nope."

"Me neither. And it looks like..." I'm still skimming through, trying to make sense of it. "It looks like he's meeting this guy today in..."

"Manchester?" says Archie in surprise, finishing my sentence as he reads over my shoulder. "But that's miles away. And, anyway, who is this Eli? And why didn't Josh tell you that's where he was going? Becks, this is weird. Keep scrolling, let's have a look."

Archie and I lean over the screen, reading through the messages, but they make no sense to me.

"What's this 'DC' they keep talking about?" I ask Archie.

"Dunno, could be someone's initials…or, I know, maybe something to do with the comics? Hey, maybe Josh has sneaked off to a comic convention."

I stare at him. "Not funny, Archie. There's something wrong. I knew it before and I was right. Do you think Josh is in trouble? I'm calling him right now."

But as I get out my phone, ready to call him, it starts ringing.

JOSH

I elbow my way through the crowd towards one of the people in uniform. I hear the words "signal failure" and "fallen tree" and "everything south of Chesterfield" and "no trains running till further notice". There's a woman handing out forms so that people can get money back on their tickets.

"Might have guessed it," says a man in a Man City shirt to my left. "What a shambles, eh? Something different every week. Last time they piled us all onto buses. Took hours. Least you get your money back though."

Everyone seems resigned to waiting around, apart from some confused-looking tourists who keep shuttling around the station, bumping their huge cases into everybody else's ankles. Then, as I watch, more of the

DELAYEDs on the departure board turn to CANCELLEDs, and an announcement I can't hear properly goes out over the tannoy. Still no one moves.

I try to do the calculation in my head. It's hard because I can't think clearly. I try to take deep breaths, but it doesn't help. If I'm delayed by an hour, even two, it will be okay, won't it? I'll still be there before the party starts.

But even if I make the party, Becky will never forgive me for leaving her to deal with everything.

I need to call her, let her know what's going on, ask her to cover for me if I'm late. But if I do call her, then she'll ask questions that, right now, I don't want to answer. If I don't though, it will only be worse later. What if I get stuck here for hours and can't get home at all?

I feel frozen to the spot. *Think it through, Josh, think it through.* There's no choice – I've got to call her.

I reach in the pocket of my hoodie for my phone. And then in my jeans pocket. And then in my bag. I'm not going to panic, I tell myself. Then I turn my bag upside down and shake everything out onto the floor, right down to the packet of biscuits that woman gave me this morning. Nothing.

I go through it all again, fumbling because my hands are shaking so much. Where can it be?

Then I realize – I must have left my phone in McDonald's.

But if I go back to try and find it, I might miss my train if it comes, or there might be an announcement or a bus or something and I won't be here.

But if I don't go, then how will I let Becky know I'm okay and not to get in a state if I'm late for the party?

And what if I never get my phone back? If I've lost it for good? I'll be in even worse trouble with Mum and Ima then.

I can't call anyone. No one knows where I am. I don't know what to do.

I stay crouched down, going through my bag one more time, unable to decide, unable to make myself get up off the floor. This is all too much. I'm just so tired. I feel sick. I've hardly eaten anything since early this morning, except some chips and a couple of biscuits.

"Are you all right, son?" says a voice above me. "Did you lose something?"

I look up and see the old man from the train this morning. The one who was giving me evils. At first, I think he's going to tell me off for making a mess, but instead, he looks like he's worried about me. I'm so surprised that I don't say anything for a moment.

I stand up. "It's nothing…it's, well, I can't find my phone and I need to call my sister and let her know I'm okay." My voice sounds breathless and high-pitched. "I'm sorry if I'm in your way."

"Now, don't you worry about that. Do you know her number?"

"Yes, but…"

He pulls the oldest phone I've ever seen out of his inside jacket pocket, and slowly turns it round in his hands. Taped to the back of it is a phone number written in spidery writing.

"It's off at the minute, but here, give me a second, let me just find this switch. Here we go, it's warming up now. That's the one good thing about these things, isn't it? Getting hold of people in an emergency. That's why my daughter made me get one. Go on, you call your sister on here." And he presses the phone into my hand.

It's stupid, but I feel tears pricking behind my eyes. I have to clear my throat before I can speak. "Are you sure?"

"Don't be daft, go on. I won't listen."

I punch in Becky's number, my heart pounding, rehearsing in my head what I'm going to tell her. Each key I press beeps loudly.

Straight to voicemail. It doesn't even ring. Perhaps Becky's on the phone. Perhaps she's trying to call me.

I hand the phone back. "Thanks, but she must be on the phone to someone else."

"Anyone else you can call?" he asks.

I can't call Mum or Ima. I just can't. Not yet. I could call Auntie Jackie, I suppose, but I don't know her number. There's no one else.

"Well, son, if you want to try again later, I'm sat just over there. I mean it. That's my wife, see." He points, and I recognize the woman from earlier too. She doesn't look any more cheerful now than she did then.

"Yes, er, I know. I think we were on the same train this morning. From London?"

He looks at me again, more closely. "Well, that's right, so you were. We were wondering how old you were. Hope you didn't think we were staring at you. Our grandson's thirteen, you see, he must be about your age. I worry about him when he's out by himself. He tells me not to though, he can look after himself, he says. Bet your folks worry about you too, eh? That's just how families are."

I nod, as he goes on. "Long way to come just for a day, isn't it? These delays don't help either. Still, better get back." He squeezes his way through the crowds to his Thermos and the seat his wife's saving for him.

I feel even worse once he's gone. I wish I had someone here with me like he does, instead of being all by myself.

BECKY

I stare at my phone in surprise for a moment. Did Josh just read my mind?

But no, it's not his name that appears, it's Ima's.

"Hi, Becks, you're there, great, this is going to be really quick. Your mum's just nipped to the loo."

It's so good to hear her voice.

"Hey, Ima, how's things? How is it all going?" I want to ask her about Josh – maybe she knows who this Eli is. But then why should I worry her when there's nothing she can do about it? So I try to sound calm.

"Fine, brilliant," she carries on at top speed. "Look, I just called Josh to let him know Denise from next door says you can borrow some extra chairs from her if you need them, but someone else answered his phone.

Said they worked at McDonald's by the station and that someone had handed in the phone there earlier today. I didn't think there was a McDonald's near the station, but never mind. Anyway, can you tell him?"

"Er, yeah, sure…"

It's probably better that she thinks he's lost his phone near Watford Junction, not, I'm guessing, near a different station in Manchester, miles away.

"Everything okay with you, Becky? Decorations looking good?"

"Yeah, except there's just one—"

"Oh, she's coming back, I've got to go, text me if you need anything, okay? Bye, love you!"

And she's gone.

While I was talking to Ima, Archie filled in Auntie Jackie on the messages and where we think Josh is. Now I tell her what Ima said about Josh having lost his phone. She sits down heavily on his bed, head in hands. Archie and I hover next to her, unsure what to do or say.

She sighs and looks up. "Have either of you got any idea what's going on with Josh?"

We shake our heads.

I feel sick inside. If only I'd talked to him the other night when he knocked on my bedroom door, instead of hiding away. I was so wrapped up in my own secret that I didn't even think that he might be hiding something too. But what can it be?

"So let's think," says Auntie Jackie. "This isn't like him, is it? We know he's normally very sensible. We know he wouldn't want to let us down. We can assume he wouldn't want us to worry and that he is still planning to be back for tonight. That *is* what he told you, isn't it, Becky?"

"Yes, well, he said he'd be back soon, but now he's lost his phone, so we can't even call him. And what about this Eli?"

"I have to be honest, that's the bit that worries me too. Are there any of his friends you could call to see if they know more about who it could be?"

"Yeah, but…Josh would be so mad if I did. He's already going to go wild that I've been on his tablet."

"Never mind that now. If he's going to be mad at someone later, then let it be me. Becky, you're doing the right thing. Use my phone, in case Josh gets his phone back and tries to call you on yours. Look, if he's not back or we haven't heard from him in another half an hour, we're going to have to tell your mums."

"But…"

"I don't want to mess up their day either, but we might have to. Anyway, let's hope it won't come to that."

Once Jackie's gone downstairs to get her phone, Archie says, "Wow, she's great, your aunt, isn't she? Proper cool head in a crisis – issuing orders all over the place, making plans. It's like we're in some police drama."

"Archie, this isn't a joke," I snap.

"I know it isn't," he says, suddenly serious again.

"I didn't want anything to spoil this party, but it's already spoiled, isn't it?" My voice cracks. "All because of my stupid, stupid brother."

"It's not spoiled," says Archie firmly, leaning down to look me in the eye. "Josh is going to walk in that door any minute and everything is going to be fine. And this will be the most spectacular fiftieth birthday party ever. All because of you. It will. I promise. Now, what can I do to help?"

"Oh, I don't know, just go and make the house beautiful."

"Your wish is my command." And he bows a ridiculous little bow and backs out of the bedroom door.

Neither Max nor Jayden have any idea where Josh is or who Eli is. No surprise there. I can tell they're laughing at me, thinking I'm making a fuss out of nothing. I hope they're right.

It only strikes me now how few real friends Josh has got. Everyone likes Josh, but hardly anyone is really close to him, I realize with a shock. For so much of our lives, it's just been him and me. And if that's true, then it's even worse that I missed what was going on.

Suddenly my phone rings again, making me jump. A number I don't recognize.

"Becky?" says the voice on the other end. There's loads of background noise, but I know instantly it's Josh. I feel a wave of relief – he's okay! – then a sharp bite of anger. I want Josh to know just how worried I've been. I want him to feel just as bad – worse, even.

"Where the hell are you?"

"I'm in Manchester…"

"I know that!"

"What? Sorry, I can't really hear you." He sounds far away, faint and, above all, utterly miserable. "I'm so sorry, Becks, I will explain, I promise. It's just, someone's lent me their phone, so I can't really talk for long. I should have been back by now, but all the trains are delayed. I'm on my way. Don't tell Mum and Ima, please. I don't know, just cover, I will be there. I'm sorry."

"Your phone," I say as loudly as I can so that he can hear me. "You left it in McDonald's…"

"What?" he shouts back. I hear what sounds like a bell chiming. "I'd better go, I think that was an announcement about my train, everyone's moving…" The line goes dead.

My mind is full of questions and I'm bursting with frustration that, right now, I can't ask Josh a single one of them. I throw the phone down angrily on the bed and punch one of the pillows. It makes me feel better to mess his things up, even a little bit. I look around the room, but there are no answers here in the folded clothes or neatly-shelved books.

I hate not knowing everything about what's going on with him and why. The only thing I do know just makes me mad: wherever he's been, whatever he's been doing, he obviously thinks it's more important than Mum or Ima, more important than me.

"Is that Josh?" mouths Auntie Jackie, poking her head round the door. She looks tired and anxious. "Can I talk to him?"

"Yeah, it was him, but he's gone."

"Already? Is he okay? What did he say? I could hear you shouting from downstairs."

She sits next to me on the bed and listens carefully while I explain as much as I know about Josh's lost phone, the train delays, and the stranger who helped him call home. He's safe and on his way home, but we don't know when he'll be back.

When I finish, she nods in a businesslike way. "Well then, some good news at least."

"Do we have to phone Mum and Ima now?" I ask.

Auntie Jackie sighs. "No, I don't think so, do you? There's no need to worry them now we know he's okay, but…" She waves her finger in the air, like she's imagining telling Josh off. "That brother of yours is going to have a *lot* of explaining to do when he gets back. Still at least he did call, finally. I wonder how he remembered your number – I mean, without his phone…"

"You know what Josh is like," I say, waving my hand in the direction of his organized shelves and tidy desk. "It would be just like him to learn our numbers off by heart or write them down or something, you know, just in case."

"Well, it's a good job he knew it, isn't it?"

"I s'pose so. But losing his phone in the first place… *that's* not like Josh at all. He's always so careful. Normally, I mean." I'm just thinking aloud now, trying to work out what's going on.

"We'll have to wait till he's home to find out more,"

says Auntie Jackie, smoothing down her skirt as she stands up. She smiles at me and shakes her head. I smile too. "Come on then, back to work."

The rest of the afternoon passes in a flash. There's so much to do. We set up the music, put up the photo gallery – which looks brilliant, I'm really proud – as well as all the other decorations, clear space in the fridge for the food and lay out the piles of plates and rows of glasses on the buffet table, leaving space for Neil's amazing birthday cake in the centre.

But whenever I do have a moment to think, I go over in my mind exactly what I'm going to say to Josh when he gets back.

The last thing to do is get changed. I put my hair up and find the silver festival glitter that Archie gave me for my birthday buried under a pile of stuff in my room.

He lies back on the bed as I wait for my nail varnish to dry. I turn round to face him.

He whistles. "You look great, Becky, amazing."

"Yeah, whatever." I shrug. "I look a mess. My hair never goes right."

"No, I'm serious." He props himself up on one elbow. "Have a proper look in the mirror. Go on."

So, reluctantly, I do. I look at my reflection for a long

time. Gone are the red eyes and wild hair from earlier. And Archie's right, I do look good – really good. I turn and smile at him.

"I'm going down to show Auntie Jackie. I think that was Neil's van pulling up a minute ago. He might need a hand with the food. Coming?"

"In a sec, just nipping to the loo."

Down in the living room, the cake's already in the centre of the table. It looks incredible, just like Ima said it would, with the chocolate layers and caramel icing. It's hard to stop myself scooping off just a little bit of the icing from the edge. I can hear voices murmuring in the kitchen, but I can't really make out the words. Well, I can make out Neil's voice and occasionally Auntie Jackie trying to get a word in. I've known Neil all my life, he's almost part of the family, but once he starts talking, it's hard to get him to stop.

I'm about to stick my head round the kitchen door when I hear him say, "Of course, if you'd asked me fifteen years ago if Ruth and Anna and I would still be friends now, well, I wouldn't have been so sure… You remember that time, Jackie, I honestly wasn't sure that our friendship would survive…"

His tone is low, confidential. I can't go in and interrupt

them now. It would look like I was eavesdropping. But I can't stop listening either. I didn't know that Ima and Mum had ever fallen out with Neil. I can't imagine it. He's so easy-going. I stand very still, barely breathing.

"Well, it's all ancient history now," says Auntie Jackie. "Something and nothing."

"Yes, but at the time—" insists Neil.

"Maybe Ruth shouldn't have asked you," interrupts Auntie Jackie, almost sharply.

"You can't blame her. I mean, it could have worked out. It was my fault. I knew she'd make a great mother, I knew they both would. But back when she and Anna were first talking about having children, it wasn't so common, was it, two women bringing up kids together. It wasn't talked about. I didn't know anyone who was doing it."

Typical Neil, making a production out of something we all already know. My mums wanted to have kids, big deal, I know the end of that story.

But then, what *did* Ima ask Neil? I wonder, confused. And what happened that was his fault? And what did any of that have to do with Mum and Ima having children?

"I just wanted to help out my friends," continues Neil. "Me being their donor seemed like the obvious solution.

I hadn't even met Sandy then, of course, let alone got married. And we spent months talking it over, thinking about what it would be like. I had all the health checks and everything. And then, well, you remember, at the last minute, I just couldn't do it. I just couldn't. When it came to it, I couldn't imagine having a child that wasn't mine, fully mine, and that's not what Ruth and Anna wanted. They wanted their own family. Two parents, that's all."

My mind is whirring. Neil could have been my dad? Seriously? I try to square this story with everything I've been told before, but just thinking about it makes my head hurt.

"Don't be too hard on yourself," says Auntie Jackie. "It was a long time ago, and who knows if it would have worked anyway. It was another three years until either of them managed to get pregnant, even at the clinic."

"But I felt I'd let them down," sighs Neil. "I *had* let them down, this was their dream. I'd agreed to help and then I broke their trust."

"But you worked through it," interrupts Auntie Jackie. "And now it's all worked out for the best, hasn't it? They got their family. You got yours. And you did stay friends after all."

Neil sighs. "You're right. Goes to show, even when you think something's broken beyond repair, there's still hope, there's still a way to fix it if you try hard enough. It just takes time. Listen to me going on… Birthdays make you think about this sort of thing, don't they?"

"I suppose so," says Auntie Jackie. "But they also make you think about how much work there is to do to get a party ready – and we're just standing round chatting! Haven't you finished that tea yet?"

I step away from the doorway quickly and back into the living room, and the voices fade to a murmur again.

This might be ancient history to Auntie Jackie, but it does still matter now, however long ago it happened, because what if Neil *had* said yes back then? Josh and I probably wouldn't exist. We wouldn't just be different people, we simply wouldn't be here at all. The thought makes me shiver.

And it's not just that. Why didn't Mum or Ima tell us? Maybe they thought that, because nothing had happened, it didn't matter. But it does.

What else aren't they telling us? Is everyone walking round with secrets? Looking like they've got nothing to hide, but with all this going on just beneath the surface? I thought I knew my family inside out, but maybe I hardly know them at all. Archie seems to know what my mums will say or do or think better than I do, and Josh… well, Josh and I never used to have secrets from each other and now it seems that we both do. Without me even noticing, everything's changed and I don't like it.

So that's it, I promise myself, enough secrets. I'll tell them all tonight.

"Hi, Becky," says Neil, coming into the living room. "You look gorgeous! So grown up! Are you all set for the party?"

I nod, unable to speak. I notice that his shoes are off and he's wearing one blue striped sock, and one black with yellow spots.

He sees me looking, grins and wanders back into the hallway to get his smart shoes. "Oh yes, I get it, I'm the one who's not ready yet." He sits down to lace them up, without stopping his flow of chat. "You've done a fantastic job with the decorations. You must have been busy. It's always like this for a function – you want to make it look effortless, right, but so much hard work has to go into making it *not* look like hard work! But this is my favourite moment – after all the prep is done, before the first guest has arrived. When anything's possible."

The doorbell rings. Archie skips down the stairs.

Auntie Jackie appears out of the kitchen, still holding the dirty mugs. "Can you two get the door?" she asks Archie and me.

And it begins.

The guests start arriving – some are people who I see all the time, others who I've never met before. The doorbell hardly stops ringing for the next half an hour. Grandma appears, with Grandpa behind her, and envelops me in a huge perfumy hug. Uncle Noah bounds in and talks about the problems on the motorway in his booming voice to anyone who'll listen. He's the only person from Ima's family who lives near enough to come to the party, so she'll be extra pleased that he's made it here despite the traffic.

So Noah's here – but what about Josh? Each time the door opens, I hope it will be him. But it never is. How much longer will he be?

There's no time to think. Just as I start to say hello to one person, answering the same questions about school and about how we managed to keep the party a surprise, someone new arrives and I start all over again. Whenever anyone asks where Josh is – which everyone does – I mumble something about how he's on his way, and encourage them to go and get a drink or to leave their presents and cards on the table.

In the middle of all the bustle, I can't help but look at every man who comes in and wonder – did they ask him? Or him? Could he have been my dad? It hits me – this must be what Josh wonders all the time. It's hardly bothered me before, but something's changed: now that I know who it *could* have been, I want to know who it *is*.

By the time Ima's text comes through – *Just leaving station. Be there in 15. Stand by* – everyone has arrived and we're all taking our places in the living room, ready to hide as soon as we hear the car pull up. Everyone except Josh. I was still hoping he'd make it, come running in at the last minute. But no. What will Mum and Ima say when they find out Josh isn't here? My stomach is fluttering, but with worry, not excitement. Worry about disappointing Mum, about not knowing what to tell Ima, about upsetting them in front of all their friends.

I'm waiting in the hallway and hear Mum's voice speaking to Ima, drifting through as the door opens.

"…dinner and a hot bath, that will suit me nicely. I feel like I've walked round the whole of London…"

I am frozen to the spot next to the door. Mum looks straight at me. She can tell instantly that something's up.

"Becky?" she asks, puzzled. "Is everything all right? What are you doing lurking here?"

I take a deep breath – there's no reason to keep this secret any longer. I fling open the door to the living room and everyone shouts at once: "HAPPY BIRTHDAY!" Mum looks absolutely stunned.

There's a moment of total silence when I wonder for the very first time, did we do the right thing?

"Oh my, Ruth – you didn't? All this…" Mum whispers, her hands held up to her face.

"Not just me," says Ima, beaming by Mum's side as she puts a glass of champagne into her hand. Ima's taking in the decorations and the food and the cake and the music and is bouncing with excitement. Mum isn't taking anything in at all. "It was Becky too, and Josh. We wanted to give you a really special birthday. One you'll never forget."

Mum looks at the glass in her hand as if she has no idea how it got there. "Yes…this is amazing. Truly amazing." And she folds me and Ima into a hug. "Thank you so much. Where's Josh so I can embarrass him with a hug too in front of all these wonderful people?"

Ima looks round the room over my shoulder.

"Er, well, he just had to nip out for something. He'll be back in a minute," I say, with my fingers crossed behind my back, hoping that will turn out to be true.

"Oh," says Mum. And her smile drops a little. "He's not here now then?" She looks tired.

I expect the inquisition from Ima about where Josh is. But instead she looks curious, not angry or worried. I guess she doesn't know what I know: that he's been out all day and we still don't know exactly where he is. I don't say anything. I don't want to spoil things for her. But my fingers are still crossed, hard, wishing that he'll come home soon.

Luckily the people hovering around us move forward and Mum is swept up in hugs and excited greetings, distracting her from asking questions about Josh – for now at least.

JOSH

The journey back is totally different from the way up. Instead of peace and quiet, it feels like hundreds of people are crammed into each carriage. I feel different too. No longer excited about meeting Eli, just feeling sick about what a mess I've got myself into.

It's obvious after about ten seconds that there's no way I'm getting a seat. By the time I get on the train, there are already people sitting in the corridors and in the luggage racks, or perched on the edges of the tables. There's barely room to move or even to breathe. I'm struggling to breathe normally anyway. My chest feels all tight, full of the things I'm worried about. My stomach's rumbling, and there's nothing I want more than the squashed biscuits in my bag – but reaching them in this crush would be impossible. There's no space. I can't even move my arm to check the time on my watch. All I know is that I'm desperately late and that I've let everyone down.

This is the only train running south, and it's stopping everywhere on its way down. So instead of speeding past fields, we're crawling through tiny local stations where a handful of people squeeze on and off each time we stop. We're moving, but painfully slowly.

The slow pace means there's plenty of time to think, which is not a good thing. Plenty of time to worry about the party and to feel bad about messing Becky around. But most of all, time to beat myself up about what I said to Eli and what he said to me. I still can't shake off the feeling that he's my brother, whether he believes it or not. It's there in the way we look, the way we act. But I don't have a way to prove it. And, despite all of that, there's this tiny voice in the back of my head, which says, *What if he's right? What if I'm just seeing what I want to see?*

When we get into Watford, I push past everyone so that I can leap off the train as soon as the doors open, nearly tripping over as I stumble onto the platform. I run through the station, weaving my way around the knots of people staring despondently up at the boards. The lights in the ticket hall are bright, but outside the station the day is fading to dusk, even though it's still warm. My hands are shaking as I fumble with my bike lock, but I eventually unlock it and cycle home as fast as I can. The blood's rushing in my ears and I can feel my heart pounding.

Even so, it's nearly eight by the time I turn the corner into our street. The party must have been going on for almost an hour already. All the lights are on in the house, and I can hear music pumping out. I know I should see if I can just slip straight in and join the party without a fuss, be nice to everyone, hope not too many people noticed I wasn't there. That would be the sensible thing to do. But I just stand there, staring. I tell myself over and over again that I need to go in and face all those people and conversations, all the noise and buzz of celebration, but my feet won't move. Instead, I want to collapse on my bed, pull the duvet over my head and not face anybody.

Finally, I move. Leaving my bike by the side of the house, I slip through the gate to the garden. There are fairy lights and coloured lanterns everywhere and streamers drifting in the trees.

"You must be Josh?" says a woman in a tight pink dress, wobbling over to me unsteadily on her high heels and clutching a glass of wine. "I studied nursing with your mum. Oh, longer ago than I care to remember. I haven't seen you since you were a baby."

I look around and realize that while everyone else in is their party clothes, I'm still wearing the jeans, hoodie and crumpled T-shirt, now stuck to my back with sweat, that I threw on at five this morning.

"Josh!" shrieks Becky. "You're here!"

She rushes up and gives me a hug so tight that it almost squeezes the breath out of me. I can tell she's pleased, no, *relieved* to see me, but her grip is so tight that she's definitely angry too. Her camera bag, slung over her shoulder, swings round and slams against my side. Pink-dress woman has disappeared.

"This looks amazing, Becks," I say once she lets me go and I can speak again. "You did all this? I mean, wow." I feel even worse about deserting her today when it's obvious how hard she's worked to make everything look perfect. Although, I don't know how much help I would have been, I mean, Becky's so much better at that sort of stuff than I am.

"I know – and you haven't even seen inside yet," she

continues. "Just shows how well I can manage without you, doesn't it?" She's staring at me, hands on hips. I can feel the stare, even without meeting her eyes. Becky's stares are legendary.

"Yeah, I know, I'm sorry about today, it's hard to explain but—"

"Look, don't think I'm forgiving you for this, not for a long time," she interrupts, "but not now, okay? Go and get changed and then go and say happy birthday to Mum at least. But later – I want to know everything. Ev-ery-thing." She pokes me in the chest with each syllable. "You so owe me."

Upstairs, I pull on a shirt and jeans and put some product in my hair. I'm starting to feel normal again. My room looks a mess because of the pile of jackets and coats on my bed from all the party guests. It's only on my way out that I realize something else is different. Not right.

I turn back and look round. The duvet's on the floor and the wardrobe door is open. And I'm sure I left my tablet on the desk and not on my bed.

So who was going through my stuff while I was out?

Becky. I feel a flash of anger. Even if she was worried about where I was, she shouldn't have gone in my room or been snooping around on my tablet, whatever the reason. I told her not to worry, didn't I? That I was okay and was coming back. After all these people have gone, she'd better say sorry.

But first I need to find Mum. Having so many people in the house makes it feel both bigger and smaller at the same time. It's hard to squeeze through the crowded rooms. Before I find Mum, Auntie Jackie finds me.

"Josh, thank god!" she exclaims. "You had us so worried. That was so thoughtless of you."

"I know," I mumble. "I'm sorry."

"Good. You should be. And what about your poor sister? It's her you need to say sorry to, not me."

Huh, I think, *Becky should say sorry to me too.*

"And your mum," continues Auntie Jackie. "Have you even seen her yet?"

"I'm just looking for her now…"

"Well, for goodness' sake, go and at least say 'happy birthday'!" She gives me a shove in the direction of the living room.

I find Mum leaning against the living-room doorframe, her head tipped to one side, listening intently to someone I don't recognize. I touch her shoulder. For a second, as she turns to me, she looks as tired as I feel, and then her face breaks into a wide grin.

"Happy birthday, Mum."

"Josh, am I glad to see you." She hugs me tight. I wince. I've only just recovered from Becky's massive hug. "Where have you been?"

I open my mouth, trying to think of something to say.

"No, never mind," continues Mum. "You can tell me all about it later when it's just us. What a day I've had! And then, this – this surprise." She lets go of me and waves her hand to take in the room and all the people. "Thank you – I know you and Becky have worked so hard. And you didn't let on at all."

"Well…" I shrug, looking at my feet. "It was mostly Becky who did the work really, not me."

Mum and I are almost the same height, so when she tilts my chin to lift it up, we are eye to eye. "You too – I know you, Josh."

"I wasn't sure you'd like it, the surprise and all the fuss and everything."

"Well…" She stretches out the word. "I was a *bit* shocked. I was looking forward to a Chinese takeaway and putting my feet up – but don't you dare tell Ima and Becky that! I would never have planned a big birthday party for myself, but now I'm here, I must admit –" she lowers her voice to a whisper – "I'm quite enjoying it.

It's not so bad being the centre of attention after all. Just as long as you and Becky are here. Nothing else really matters."

Out of nowhere, Ima appears behind me and throws her arm round my shoulder. "So, the wanderer returns…" she says cheerfully. I'd expected her to be angry that I wasn't here when they got home, but instead she seems very relaxed. I know Ima loves a party – tonight's as much for her as it is for Mum, maybe even more.

"Yeah, uh, I…"

"Not the best time to choose to go and get your phone though, Josh. I mean, you had all afternoon, and instead you disappear off at the crucial point and miss the big moment!"

"My phone?"

"Yes, of course. It was hours ago I called Becky and told her where you'd lost it. Although I guess you were too busy preparing for the party to go any earlier. You're lucky someone found it."

"Er, yeah, right."

"And did you get the message about Denise's chairs in the end? It's a good job that you didn't borrow them after all, it's just fine as it is. It would have been too crowded in here with any more furniture."

Denise? Chairs? Knowing where my lost phone is? Nothing Ima is saying makes any sense, it's like she's speaking a different language. All I can do is nod and hope that Becky will fill me in later.

"Oh, Anna, look," exclaims Ima, catching hold of Mum's arm. "Paula's brought her new girlfriend, they weren't sure she'd be able to make it, come on, let's go over."

Mum looks back and raises her eyebrows at me in mock resignation, as Ima sweeps her away, but she's grinning too. She looks like she's having a good time.

I wander back into the kitchen. I want to keep out of the way so that Becky or Auntie Jackie won't find me and have a go. This seems like a safe place. At least it's quieter in here and cooler. I start to relax, relief flooding through me: I did it. I met Eli. I got back okay in the end despite everything going wrong. I did it all by myself. And everyone else did fine without me. They didn't need me. Maybe they even got on better with me out of the way. Anyway, I'm at the party now, aren't I? It's sorted. It's all going to be okay.

Except I don't feel too good, my head's aching and I feel a bit sick. I hardly slept last night and I still haven't eaten anything since lunchtime. But, I can't be bothered to move, even to get some food. I'll just sit here, till I feel a bit better, and let the party happen around me.

But I don't start feeling better. Instead, I feel worse. I start thinking about how Becky went through my stuff, and how angry I am with her. Not just with her, Auntie Jackie too, for telling me off like I'm a little kid. And Mum and Ima, for not even thinking about how *I* might feel about not having a dad. And Eli, for calling me crazy and walking away. And the donor, whoever he is, for not being here. And with me, for just taking it all and saying nothing. But now I've had enough. I'm angry with everyone now. I can feel it building up inside me till I can hardly breathe. It's all right for them. They all know who they are and where they come from, they all seem so sorted. Except me. It's not fair.

Whenever someone comes in, I just sit there silently and listen as they tell me how they know Mum or nod along as they ask me about school. But luckily they never stay long, no one's much interested in a thirteen-year-old boy, they just want to catch up with old friends and shriek over how young everyone looks in the photos.

I steer well clear of the embarrassing dancing – I so don't want to get dragged into that – but when I finally leave the kitchen to go to the loo, I catch a glimpse of

Becky dancing with Archie – her skirt flying, the glitter sparkling on her face, her hair coming loose with curls escaping, head thrown back laughing. She looks so happy. So free.

BECKY

And then it's over.

The last people are getting their coats and looking for their car keys. Some left early – because of babysitters or long journeys home – others almost need pushing out of the door. Archie went home an hour ago with his mum, after she stopped in for a drink and to say happy birthday to Mum.

"Message me," he whispered in my ear as we hugged goodbye. "I want to know the whole story. Are you sure you don't want me to stay over, so I'm here when you tell your mums?"

"No, but I will tell you everything, I promise."

Once the last guest has waved goodbye, Mum turns the music off and shuts the French windows. The silence rings in my ears. The house feels huge and empty. It's just the four of us – and Auntie Jackie – left.

"It's so late. We should all go to bed, especially you two," says Ima, stifling a yawn, but she doesn't move from her spot on the sofa. No one else stirs either. Her head is leaning on Mum's shoulder and they both have their shoes off and their feet up on the coffee table. Now that we've stopped, none of us can summon up the energy to move again. I'm too keyed up to sleep anyway. I can feel the pressure building in my chest from the words I've been waiting to say.

"All those people," sighs Mum. "Some I haven't even *thought* about in years. You must have spent ages chasing them up. Sadie looks just the same though, doesn't she?"

"Uh huh." Ima nods. "Not like Peter. Old and fat now, I hardly recognized him."

"Nothing wrong with old and fat. I'm old and fat now too," says Mum sleepily.

"No, you're not," I protest.

"Old and fat," she says again, not really listening to me. "But wise too, remember. It's good to have lived a bit. And good to celebrate it."

Auntie Jackie is still on her feet and, unlike the rest

of us, looking as fresh and smart as she did at the beginning of the evening.

"Never mind the mess, we can sort all of that in the morning," she says.

"It *is* the morning," corrects Mum.

"After we've been to bed, I mean. Anyone want a final cup of tea? Or hot chocolate? I'll get the kettle on."

"Hot chocolate sounds perfect," says Ima, as Mum and I nod in agreement. "And is there any of that cake left? I'm not quite sure I'm old and fat *enough* yet, to be honest, and I'm sure another slice of that cake will help. It's out of this world."

"There's a little bit. I'll bring in the plate and some spoons," says Jackie. "Josh, what about you?"

Josh is slumped in our old squashy armchair, his legs hanging over one of its arms. His eyes are shut, but I think he's still awake. Just. He doesn't speak or open his eyes, only shakes his head.

"Did you have a good day, Mum?" I ask when Auntie Jackie puts the tray of mugs down on the coffee table.

"I had an unforgettable day," she says, rubbing her eyes. "A day full of surprises. I feel very lucky."

"It's just, well, as we're all here, there's something I'd like to tell you all."

"Oh?" says Mum, smiling. "Is this yet another birthday surprise?"

At exactly the same time, Ima leans forward and says, "What? What is it, Becky?" in a worried voice.

Josh opens his eyes, suddenly alert. He thinks I'm about to tell on him to Mum and Ima. "It's late, I'm going to bed," he says, swinging his feet down and sliding forward in his chair. So, before he can go anywhere, I have to blurt it out.

"Josh, hold on." He hovers reluctantly, so I keep going. "I don't know if it is a surprise exactly." I look over at Ima. "It's nothing to worry about. And I'm not in trouble. It's…" I take a deep breath. "I'm gay."

Once I've said the words, everything seems to stop, like someone has pressed the *pause* button or muted the volume. The silence feels like it's going to go on for ever.

I can't stand it when no one says anything, so I start talking again just to fill up the silence. "There, that's all. Just thought you'd like to know. I haven't got a girlfriend or anything in case you were wondering."

Still no one says anything.

"This is the bit where you all say how much you still love me, and then we can go to bed."

"Of course, of course we love you, Becks," says Ima,

shaking her head. "But are you *sure* you're gay? I mean, you're only thirteen. You don't have to know now, there's plenty of time to work things out. It's just, I never thought…but how likely is it?"

No one's crashed their car at the announcement, but I'd hoped for something better than this. Perhaps I imagined we'd all have a giant group hug, like in a TV drama, and say how much we loved each other. But that was a stupid idea. That's not real life.

Instead, Ima doesn't even sound like she believes me. She doesn't even trust me to know my own mind. But she, out of everyone, should understand that I'm not making this up.

"What do you mean, 'likely'?" I ask Ima. "It's not 'likely'. It just is."

"I want you to be sure. I mean, don't rush into anything, I don't want you to make your life harder. I want you to be happy."

Everything about today has been too much: the early start, the late night, the worries about Josh, the overheard conversation between Neil and Auntie Jackie. All too much. I can feel all the fear and anger and worry bubbling away inside me, and now it's overflowing. I've had enough.

"What?" I shout. "And does happy mean being straight? I don't believe you're saying this!"

I'm too angry to stay still, so I get up and start pulling down some of the decorations. "You're not thinking about me. This is about you. Just because it was hard for you, doesn't mean it's going to be hard for me. Things are different now. It's not the Dark Ages any more, like when you were young. I thought you'd be *pleased*. But you're not – you're just like Archie's mum, you're just like everyone else."

"Becky, come on, listen, that wasn't what I meant..." Ima comes over and puts her hand on my shoulder, but I shake it off. "I just worry about you. You might lose friends or not be able to do all the things you want to. People still say hateful things, you know."

"Be quiet, Ruth," says Mum firmly, turning to Ima. "Just be quiet. Becky's right. It's different for her generation. It doesn't matter so much today."

"Maybe not so much, but it's still there," Ima says. She touches Mum's arm. "You don't know this, Anna, but when I asked Carli's mum if they wanted to come to the surprise party—"

"You did what? When?" I exclaim.

"It was when I picked you up from their fancy house,

223

you must have still been upstairs." Ima waves her hand. "It doesn't matter when. The point is I invited her and she was all smiles – right until the moment she realized I had a wife and not the husband she assumed I did. Then suddenly, she said they had other plans."

"Okay," says Mum. "I'm not saying that these things don't still happen and, yes, it might not always have been easy for us, but look, now we've got our home, our family, our work. We even got married. I mean, who would have thought that ever could have happened?"

The look between them is so intense that I have to turn away. It's like I'm not here any more, like this is no longer about me at all.

"I know," says Ima, slumping back down onto the sofa, head in hands. "I just thought we could prove them wrong, that's all."

"Prove who wrong?" I ask. Now I'm more confused than angry.

"Life's not a competition," says Mum. "It doesn't matter what other people say, what they think. No one else gets to decide the right way to be us, only us."

"What are you talking about?" I say again.

Ima sighs. "Okay. We knew there were other same-sex couples having kids when we first started talking about

224

becoming parents. But we didn't know any personally. Not even one. So we always felt we had to prove ourselves at every step, you know, be the best parents possible, better than any straight couple, perfect. We had to be mother, father, everything. My family made it clear pretty early on that they wanted very little to do with us, all of them except Noah. It's not been easy for him either, caught between us. For my parents, well, even if they lived nearer, I'm not sure how much we'd see them. I think they care more about what people think than about their own daughter's happiness or getting to know their grandchildren." She sounds sad, but angry too.

"But that's not going to happen to me," I protest. "Things are totally different now." And, I think but don't say, it's different because *you're* my parents and you're gay. If anyone should understand, if anyone should be there no matter what life throws at me, it should be *you*.

Ima carries on, almost like she hasn't heard me.

"That made us more determined for you not to miss out on anything. People would still make comments though. Comments about how having no dad would stop you being able to relate to men, or that having gay parents would make a child gay. All nonsense. I thought we could show them they were wrong." She sighs again. "I know,

now that I say it out loud, it sounds so ridiculous."

"*I'm* straight," says Josh. His voice is hoarse. "You don't have to worry about me."

I spin round to look at him, my arms full of tattered streamers. "Thanks, Josh, that really helps, you know." I hope he realizes how sarcastic I'm being.

"Becky and Josh," says Mum slowly. "You two are the best thing to ever happen to us. We are so proud of you both. This news *did* come as a bit of a surprise, Becky, but maybe that's because we should have been paying closer attention to what's going on in your life. I bet it wasn't a surprise to you, was it?" she asks softly.

I shake my head. "At first it was. But I think that was only cos I'd been trying to ignore my feelings. I didn't *want* to tell you right away. I didn't want you to think, I don't know, that I was copying you or something. I didn't want any hassle." I glare at Ima, who looks away. "But then I did want to tell you. Because I didn't want to keep secrets any more. But perhaps I was right first time. I never should have said anything."

I'm still angry but beginning to calm down. Until Josh opens his big mouth.

"But what about me, Becks?" he interrupts. "You could have talked to me. Why the big secret?"

I can't believe that *he's* making out like *I'm* the one keeping secrets, when he's the one with something to hide. I don't care any more about whether he gets into trouble or not. I've had enough.

JOSH

As soon as I say the words, I know I've made a big mistake. The biggest. All the attention has been on Becky. Now suddenly it's on me.

When Becky's angry, it's best just to ignore her and wait until the storm's over, but I'm not thinking clearly right now. My head's pounding. I'm so tired. It feels like today has gone on for ever and it's never going to end. I'm certainly not ready for an argument.

"Oh," says Becky, pointing at me, her eyes flashing. "Oh, so *you're* the one to talk about secrets, are you? Everything about *your* life is an open book, is it?"

"Becky...please..." I groan. But I know what's coming.

"So *you* weren't off all day today, without telling

228

anyone where you were going, in Manchester meeting some stranger off the internet?"

Becky's leaning over me now. I get to my feet shakily, so that we're face to face, eye to eye. I remember how angry I am with her, with everybody.

"Shut up, Becky! How do you know I was in Manchester? How do you know what I was doing? Eh? The only way you know is cos you went snooping through my stuff."

"Yeah, and so what? Wouldn't you have done the same? I was *worried* about you. I wanted to know if you were okay. And you landed me in it. You expected me to cover for you, without even bothering to tell me why." Her voice is on the point of cracking. We're both shouting now.

"Stop! Both of you!" shouts Mum. We turn to look at her. If Mum loses her cool, then you know it's serious. "Everyone *sit* down and let's talk about this like normal people. Now, what is this, Josh? What's Becky talking about? You weren't here today?"

"Not exactly, not all day," I say. Becky snorts. "It doesn't matter. I'm here now."

"I think it does matter actually. It matters a lot," Ima says crisply. "And what's this about meeting someone off the internet? That's serious – unless your mum is going to tell me I'm overreacting about that as well."

"Of course not," says Mum. "But first I think Josh needs to tell us what's going on."

"It wasn't like that, it's not how it sounds. I was perfectly safe."

"So what *was* it like?" says Mum.

"Look, I was chatting to someone in this online group—"

"What, you mean Becky's right?" cries Ima, throwing her hands in the air. "Have we taught you nothing? Anything could have happened to you! Anything!"

"What sort of group?" asks Mum.

"Okay, I'll tell you, but you're not to be angry."

"I think it's a bit late for that," chips in Auntie Jackie. She's been so quiet that I'd forgotten she was still here. Mum even manages a weak smile. "You need to tell us, Josh."

"I joined this group. It's for people like me who are…"

I look around at their faces, all turned towards me. Mum and Ima listening anxiously, Becky looking more confused than angry now, Auntie Jackie leaning calmly against the door. My family.

"…people who are donor-conceived and are looking

for the rest of their families," I carry on without looking up. "It's just a chat group really, but then I found this guy, Eli. And I think – I mean, I *thought*…oh, I don't know – that he might be my brother. Don't you see? I had to meet him. I had to find out."

"Whoa, that's enough," says Ima. "What on earth have you been doing? Scouring the web for some stranger who might happen to have some of the same genes as you? Are you serious? He could have been anybody. I can't believe you would be so stupid."

"And this was in Manchester? You went to Manchester to meet him? Today?" asks Mum, still confused.

"Manchester, London, Timbuktu, who cares? I went to meet him. We talked. We had a McDonald's. You wouldn't have known if the trains hadn't been delayed. That's all. It's not like I've been recruited into some criminal gang or been doing drugs or something. Why can't you just leave it?"

"But, Josh, I don't get it," says Mum. She leans in and, even though I don't want to, I can see the hurt in her eyes. I quickly turn away. "I'm sorry, but I don't. All this sneaking around… How could you ever think that was a good idea? Why didn't you just talk to us? If this really matters to you, we could have talked about it.

I'm sure there are plenty of ways to find out more about your donor if that's what you really want. We could have done it together."

"But we never *do* talk about it, do we? We talk about everything else, but no one *ever* even mentions the donor. The person who's our dad." Mum winces at the word "dad", just for a moment, but enough for me to notice. "It's like you told us the story when we were kids, and then that was that, we all moved on. Except I don't want to move on. I'm old enough to know *now*."

There's a moment when I think Mum's going to agree, when she's going to reach over and stroke my hair and tell me it's all going to be okay.

Instead, she just shakes her head and says quietly, "We've been working too much. Perhaps if I'd been around more, listened more…"

Ima turns to Mum, even angrier now.

"Anna, that's got nothing to do with it. This isn't *your* fault. Right now, Josh isn't behaving like he's old enough to be trusted with anything – sneaking round behind our backs, putting himself at risk, letting his sister down…"

"What about *you* letting *me* down?" I shout. "I've got a right to know who my dad is, who *I* am. You don't understand what it's like being the only guy in the family, you just don't get it and never will, and now I might have a brother and all you want to do is stop me seeing him."

Suddenly everyone starts talking at once. My head feels like it's going to explode.

"Okay, okay," says Mum, cutting through the noise. "There's a lot to take in here. Let's stop now, before we get even more upset. We can talk about this tomorrow when we're calmer. We all need some sleep."

"But, Anna—"

"It's my birthday," says Mum wearily. "At least, it *was* my birthday an hour or so ago, so you all have to listen to me. And I say it's bedtime – now go."

"See what I mean?" I mutter to Becky, breathing deeply to stop the tears coming. "They *still* won't talk about it." But really I'm glad that Mum has put a stop to all the shouting.

We each brush our teeth and get ready for bed, not speaking, barely acknowledging each other's presence. Auntie Jackie's sleeping in Becky's room, so Becky's on a mattress on the floor in mine, where there's more space. When I click the light off, I can hear her breathing, just like we're kids again in our matching beds.

I thought I was too worked up to sleep, but as soon as my head lands on the pillow, I can feel my eyes closing.

I'm starting to drift off when Becky whispers, "Josh? You awake?"

"Yeah. You?"

"Course I am. You really went looking for a brother?" she says quietly. Her voice sounds small, not like Becky at all. All the anger I felt towards her has gone. "You went looking for your brother, *our* brother, and you didn't tell me?"

"I didn't think you'd want to know. You always said it didn't matter. So I thought I'd go and find out stuff by myself." I pause and stare into the darkness, looking for the right words. It's easier to say what I mean, knowing that she can't see me. "Then I could surprise you, see. I thought when you knew there was a real person, not just some dream of mine, then you'd care. It was for you too, honestly. I was going to tell you."

Becky's silent, but I know she's listening.

"I thought, perhaps you thought we weren't enough, you and me, so you went looking for someone else."

Suddenly, I realize she's totally misunderstood everything. My words start tumbling over each other as I try to explain. "I wasn't looking for a brother, I was looking for our donor and I couldn't work out how to find him, but I saw Eli's picture, and he looked so much

234

like me that I thought we *must* be related. Honestly, I'll show you. But anyway…I messed it up. I don't know what I think any more. I told him I thought we were brothers and he didn't believe me. He doesn't want anything to do with me now."

"Oh, Josh, I'm sorry." She sounds like she really means it.

I swallow. "It's okay for you. You've got me, *and* you've always got friends too – Archie, Carli, people who really get you. It's not like having to hang out with guys like Jayden or Max. It's so easy for you. I just thought maybe Eli would be…" I tail off.

"Well," she sighs. "It's not just you who's messed things up. I've messed it all up with Carli too."

"Oh," I say eventually, everything slowly fitting into place. "You and Carli?"

"Me and Carli nothing. I wish there was."

Another silence.

"So my sister's a lesbian? Really?"

"Yeah, reckon so." Becky's voice is slow, sleepy.

"That's cool. It'll take a bit of getting used to though. Being even more outnumbered."

"Ha, you'll survive."

Silence. Becky's breathing gets slower. Just like when

we were little, I don't want her to go to sleep and leave me on my own.

"Becky?"

"Mmm…?"

"What are we going to do?"

"Right now? Nothing. Sleep."

"Are we okay?"

"You and me? Yeah, we're okay. Night."

As my body finally relaxes into sleep, I know she's right. For the first time in a long time, we're okay again.

"Night."

BECKY

It's warm and bright when I wake up, which means it's late. For a moment, I'm not sure where I am. Josh is still asleep, arms flung back, the way he always sleeps, as if someone's dropped him on the bed from a great height. I was too tired last night to take the glitter off my face, so I start picking chunks of it off now with my nails. Josh is going to have a go about the mess in his room, but I don't care.

I sit up and everything about yesterday comes back in a rush – Josh disappearing, finding out that Neil could have been our dad, the party, telling people I'm gay for the first time, Josh's wild idea that we have a brother out there somewhere. All the secrets tumbling out, one after another. It's too much. I slump back down under the duvet.

When I wake up again, it's even later. My mouth's dry and I'm ravenous. Josh has gone, leaving the bed neatly made behind him. But as I reach out for my phone, I notice someone has left a cup of tea on the floor next to my pillow. Josh? Mum? Ima? Even though it's barely lukewarm, I sip it gratefully and scroll through my messages, putting off the moment I need to go downstairs.

They are all from Archie, asking how it went with telling Mum and Ima. But the final one says:

Emergency meeting!! My house. 3. Can u
& Josh come?!

I sigh – always such drama with Archie. But I am intrigued. What's going on? I get up and shower, letting the hot water wake me up before I have to speak to anyone.

Downstairs looks good. Tidier than normal. Auntie Jackie must have done it. All the photos are in a neat pile on the kitchen table and empty bottles stacked tidily by the recycling bin. Mum's at the sink, washing up glasses. Josh is eating a sandwich at the kitchen table. The radio's on quietly and, even though no one's talking, there's a feeling like a conversation has just finished and the words are still hanging in the air.

"You shouldn't have to wash up after your own party," I say, grabbing a tea towel and starting to dry the glasses.

"Becky, you're up," Mum says, turning from the sink. "Jackie just left for the drive home, but we didn't want to wake you. I hope that was the right thing to do."

"Yeah, thanks." I yawn. "I needed the sleep. Look, if I help with the washing-up now, can I go over to Archie's later?"

"Sure. We're almost done here anyway. Josh has sorted out the garden." She nods over at him and Josh looks up at me sheepishly. Even though he's trying to make up for it now, he knows how bad he should feel about abandoning me yesterday.

"Josh, you coming too?"

There's a pause. No one says anything. I look from Josh to Mum and back again.

"Well…" says Mum.

"Come on, isn't it enough that I'm banned from going online? Now I'm not allowed to see my friends either?" he says.

"Josh, you're in no position to argue," says Mum sternly.

"Oh, Mum, go on," I plead. "Archie wants him to come over too."

I can tell she's weakening. Mum doesn't like being

angry. She likes everything to be smoothed over, and everyone to be comfortable and happy.

"Anyway," says Josh glumly, "perhaps I should get out of Ima's way."

"All right then," says Mum. "Go on, go."

On the walk to Archie's house, Josh is really quiet.

"What's that about not going online?" I ask, as we turn out of our road.

"Ima's taken my tablet. She's keeping it for two weeks or till I show I can be trusted again." I can imagine Ima's voice saying those exact words. "I'm only allowed it to do homework. And I haven't got my phone. That's still in Manchester and I've got no idea how to get it back. It's grim. I'm surprised all the shouting didn't wake you up. Just before you came down, Ima went off to do some yoga to try and calm down."

"Two weeks? That's so unfair." I try to sound outraged, but really I think Josh has got off lightly for what he did. "Maybe they'll change their minds sooner."

"Maybe," he says gloomily. It's clear he doesn't want to talk about it any more. "So what's this about with Archie?"

"Don't know – 'emergency meeting', he said."

"What does that even mean?" mutters Josh.

We walk on in silence for another few minutes. My mind is whirring.

"Look, I've been thinking," I say finally. "If you still want to find our donor, well, I want to too. I want us to do it together. Properly."

"Really?" Josh's face lights up. "You think it's a good idea?"

"Well, it's not the *worst* idea you've ever had. And, well, something happened yesterday. I overheard something…"

I tell him about what Neil said, and his eyes get wider and wider.

"So he could even be someone we know? Wow. I hadn't even thought of that."

"I don't know. I don't think so. That wasn't what it sounded like from Neil. I don't think Mum and Ima asked anyone else after him. But it made me think. For the first time, the donor felt like a real person, not just someone in a story. I still don't need him, I don't feel like there's anything missing. But, okay, maybe I do want to know who he is and if we've got brothers or sisters too. But no more secrets. We've got to get Mum and Ima on side first."

"I can't imagine getting Ima on side about anything right now," he says as we reach Archie's house. "She's being so unfair."

I ring the bell.

"Maybe if she does enough yoga, she'll chill out and everything will be okay…" I press my fingers together, stand on one leg and start chanting "Om" in an attempt to make Josh smile.

Archie's so quick to get to the door that I can still hear the doorbell playing a tune behind him. He looks at my yoga position, shakes his head and hustles us in quickly, like we're secret agents on the run in a spy film.

"Mum's out. The Little Horror's upstairs. Come in."

The living room's already full of people I didn't expect to see here. Kai is leaning back in Archie's mum's favourite chair, the one with the pop-up footrest, with Olivia perched on the arm. Alex and Carli are sitting awkwardly at either end of the huge leather sofa. Kris is sitting on the floor, leaning back against Alex's legs. Carli's face is all red and puffy, like she's been crying, but she looks up and smiles as we come in. I want to hug her. The urge to reach out for her and make it all okay is so strong, like something inside me is pulling me towards her. But I don't. Instead I look at Archie, confused. What's going on?

Josh takes the armchair, so, rather than squash between Alex and Carli, I sit on the floor, leaning against the wall.

"It's about the Pride group," says Carli, all in a rush. "My parents read some of the messages on my phone and found out I was part of the group – and now they've said I can't go any more."

"They read your messages?" exclaims Kai. "That's awful."

Everyone's staring at Carli now, waiting for her to go on.

"Yeah, but worse than that, I overheard them talking when they thought I'd gone to bed – they're going to complain to the school. My mom's going in later this week to meet Ms Bryant. She wants to get the group shut down. She says it's immoral and corrupting and it shouldn't be happening in school. What if they listen to her? Then I've spoiled everything for everyone. That's the last thing I wanted, to make things worse. She doesn't know I've come to meet you now. She thinks I'm studying with Olivia. I'm so sorry."

As Carli talks, a cold feeling takes hold inside me. All the stuff she'd said before about her mum's "traditional views" flashes back into my mind. But Carli always played it down, like it wasn't really that serious. Now I know that someone can be as polite and friendly as Carli's mum and still think horrible things, like that I'm immoral and corrupting just because I'm gay. She can believe that something about me is so awful that she wants her daughter to have nothing to do with people like me. It makes my stomach churn. I can tell Archie feels the same way. Kai and Olivia and Alex probably do too. She might not have been talking about us personally, but it still feels like we're being judged.

"See," says Archie, looking round at the serious faces in the room. "That's why I thought we needed an emergency meeting."

"First of all," says Alex, "this isn't your fault, Carli, okay? None of it." Archie nods vigorously. "It sounds pretty rubbish for you at home right now, and no one here blames you. I mean, this shouldn't be a huge surprise – that's kind of why we need a Pride group, right, because not everyone thinks it's okay to be LGBTQ. Of *course* some people aren't going to like it."

"But what if the school does get scared and decides to stop the group? They could, couldn't they? And we've only just started. We've got so many ideas. What if that all gets trashed?" Archie's voice is rising.

"I mean, my mom knows how to make a fuss," breaks in Carli. "She might make out like she's all calm and quiet, but she can be really determined. She knows how to say all the things that make teachers worried." She fiddles with her bracelet, twisting it round her wrist one way and then the other.

Everyone goes quiet.

But I must be the quietest and palest out of them all. Because it's my fault. I was the one who encouraged Carli to come to Pride group, who desperately wanted her to be there. If I hadn't asked her, then she wouldn't have come, then she wouldn't be in trouble with her parents now and none of this would have happened. I feel awful for her. And for all of us, especially Archie. The group matters so much to him.

Alex finally breaks the silence, but even he doesn't sound like he totally believes what he's saying.

"Look, it will be okay. Ms Bryant's got our backs. We've done all the right things. Loads of schools do this. The governors have approved it. And, come on, what harm are we doing? Really? We're just a group of kids, talking, supporting each other, having a laugh and eating cake. It's not like we're, I don't know, giving out condoms in the corridors…"

"Or plotting a queer takeover of the school," chips in Kai.

"Or having a kiss-in outside the science blocks," adds Archie.

"Or forcing everyone to drape themselves in rainbow flags," continues Olivia.

"Or to listen to k.d. lang," I say.

"What's k.d. lang?" asks Kai.

"She's this lesbian singer from ages ago," explains Josh. "Our mums have all her albums. I reckon you'd like her."

"I suppose you're right," says Carli quietly. "But, oh, I don't know. Perhaps I should just stop coming to the group. It's not even *for* me – I'm not LGBTQ. I just wanted to hang out with you guys, show some support, y'know. You're my friends. But it's all backfired. I made it worse. If I just left it would be easier for you. Maybe my parents would lay off."

"No!"

It comes out louder than I mean it to and everyone turns to look at me. "Why should you? You're part of the group, just as much as anyone else. Anyway, it's got to work so that people can come no matter what their parents say, otherwise what's the point of having the group at all? We can't just give up."

Carli meets my eyes and smiles at me gratefully. No matter how much I try to pretend it doesn't, that smile still makes my stomach flutter. I'm concentrating on trying to stop blushing when Josh starts talking.

"I get it, Carli. I'm not LGBTQ either, but it's different for me. There's loads of times I wish I could walk away, that I didn't have gay parents, and that I had a mum and a dad like you're supposed to." He looks up at me. "I know, Becks, I'm not, like, proud of thinking that, but it's true."

"What?" I ask. "I didn't say anything."

But that's the thing with Josh, it doesn't matter what I say or don't say, he knows what I'm thinking anyway.

"It would be so much easier not to have to watch people to see how they are going to react, not to explain stuff and answer stupid questions all the time. It's so boring – but I can't walk away. And I don't want to, not really, not from *anyone* in my family." He looks over at me again. "But, Carli, you can just go, and maybe you will. But I hope you stick around, cos that's the best thing you could do."

"But what are we going to *do*?" asks Archie, looking back at Alex with wide eyes. Yuck, I hope I never look quite as dopey about Carli or anyone.

"I'll go and see Ms Bryant," Alex says. "I'll talk to her about the group and how important it is. Even if Carli's parents complain, that's only one family. She's got to listen to us too."

"It's not just up to her though, is it?" I say. "She's not going to want to get into trouble either. It's not enough to tell her. It can't just be us. We need to *show* the governors and everyone that the whole school supports us. I wonder…"

An idea's starting to take shape in my mind, like a photograph gradually coming into focus. Something we can do that involves everyone. Something visual. Something that no one can miss.

"What, Becks?" asks Archie. Everyone's turned away from Alex now and is looking at me.

So I start to explain my idea.

JOSH

We spend the rest of Sunday afternoon at Archie's. It's far better than being at home. Once we finish planning, Kai googles k.d. lang, and before long we're watching YouTube clips of the nineties, singing along and laughing at the clothes and hairstyles.

Then I spot Carli checking the football scores on her phone, and we get Archie to put the TV on for the match. Archie raids his mum's snack cupboard and soon we're all eating crisps, drinking Coke and shouting at the TV. When Archie's little brother Mark sticks his head round the door to see what's going on, Archie doesn't tell him to go away like he usually does. Mark's delighted that he's allowed to join in.

Carli and Becky still aren't really talking, but they

keep looking over at each other and then looking away again. It's strange to think about Becky fancying Carli. It takes a whole load of readjusting in my head. But instead of making things more confusing like I thought it would, it all makes much more sense.

I hope they're going to be friends again – it turns out happy, overexcited, loud Becky is better than miserable, cross, silent Becky. I know which one I'd rather be living with.

I have such a good time at Archie's that it's not till we're walking home that I remember about Eli and the donor and the mess I'm in. The one good thing is that it's not a secret any more – Becky's going to help – but I don't see how much the two of us can really find out, even together.

I'm still in a daze by the time I get into school on Monday morning. I'm trying to put things in order in my mind, but it feels like there's too much to think about all at once.

I'm so out of it that I don't even notice Jayden running up behind me until he slaps me on the back.

"Hey," he puffs, leaning over to catch his breath.

I keep on walking. "Hey."

"So what was all that about at the weekend?"

"All *what* about?"

"You know, you disappearing, Becky phoning me trying to track you down. Something about someone called Eli?"

"What?"

"Where were you? Obviously up to something you didn't want Becky to know." He nudges me with his elbow. "Plus you didn't come to football. And you haven't replied to any messages all weekend. Why didn't you let us in on it? Come on, spill."

"Oh, that," I say, trying to come up with a good excuse. "Nothing really, just a mistake. I lost my phone – I've still not got it back – and my mum needed something at home, that's all. You know, just parents worrying about nothing."

"Sure? Really?" Jayden looks disappointed. "I thought it was going to be something interesting. I thought you were in loads of trouble or you'd sneaked off with Carli or something."

"No, sorry."

He shoots me a disbelieving look. "You've been really weird this term, Josh. Really weird." And then he walks off.

When I spot Carli at break time and see Archie in

English they look as anxious as I feel. The day flies by. Becky tries to find some of the others from photography club at lunchtime to see what they think about our plan, while Alex gets word round the rest of the Pride group.

And when the bell goes at the end of the school day, there's a whole crowd of us gathered in the lower corridor. A couple of people have brought friends, so there's even more people than there were at the last meeting.

Alex knocks, and Ms Bryant shouts, "Come in!" She looks surprised as, one after another, we all file into her classroom.

"A delegation?" she says, raising her eyebrows. "To what do I owe the honour?"

Ms Bryant's not a scary teacher, but she's got a very dry sense of humour and doesn't like people wasting her time.

We look at each other nervously. Silence. Then several people all start talking at once. We'd decided to come and see Ms Bryant, but not what to say when we got here. We don't even know if Carli's mum has already been into school to see her.

"Okay," says Ms Bryant, holding up her hand to quieten us down. "Sit down, all of you. Alex, go on, you go first. I'm all ears."

"We wanted to talk about the Pride group," Alex says. "We're worried that…I mean, we heard that…well, that perhaps some people aren't happy with us meeting and because of that maybe the school won't want to support the group any more."

"Ah," Ms Bryant says, closing the book she was marking and adding it to the pile on her desk. "I see."

"And so we thought if we could show everyone just how important the group is and why it matters so much for LGBTQ students – well, for everyone really – then we'd be safe."

"Not just safe," Becky butts in. "I mean, it's fine meeting in a classroom, hidden away, that's safe, but that's not enough, is it? It's called the Pride group, right, so we should be proud."

Ms Bryant leans back in her chair and looks round at our worried faces. "So why are you telling me this now? I agree with you, be proud, be out there. The only thing to remember is that not everyone might be ready for that yet. I mean, they might feel safe in the group but not ready to be out in public. That's okay too. And, anyway, you're already doing it – look at all the plans you've made – an assembly at the end of term, that's being proud, that's really visible. If you're worried that you don't have support from the school, then take it from me, you do." Her voice quietens. "I do understand how important this is."

"So, if someone's parents complained…" asks Carli nervously.

"Then we'd talk about it with them, we'd listen, we'd work something out together. It's a three-way partnership at Larkhall – teachers, parents and students – you know that. But that's for me to worry about, not you."

"The assembly…" says Becky. "That's brilliant, but it's not for ages. There's something else we want to do, something this week."

"This week?" says Ms Bryant. "Okay, tell me about it."

"Well, it's IDAHOBIT this week…"

"That's the International Day Against Homophobia, Biphobia, Interphobia and Transphobia on the seventeenth of May," explains Kai eagerly. I notice they've got even more badges than usual on their blazer today.

"Thanks, Kai," says Ms Bryant drily. "I'm up to speed now."

So we explain what we'd like to do, how we've thought it all through and that we wouldn't need any help. Ms Bryant tries to suggest that we take more time to plan it properly, to give it a few weeks, bring some more people on board, but eventually she realizes that we've made up our minds.

"Go on then," she says. "And good luck. You know, I'll be first in line."

BECKY

"I don't see why we had to get up so early," grumbles Josh as we walk into school together. "We don't have to get anything ready till lunchtime."

I've been awake for ages and desperate to get out of the house. I practically had to drag Josh out though. I hope he's not getting cold feet about today.

Things are gradually thawing with Josh and Ima – maybe she and Mum have been talking things over or the yoga's calming her down – but even so, it's been a strange atmosphere at home since the weekend.

I'm not sure what Mum and Ima would think about what we're doing today. I hope they'd be pleased if they knew, but, by doing this, we've created a whole new secret without meaning to. That's why I just wanted to get up and go. To be doing rather than thinking.

Mum and Ima have always been clear: our family's nothing to be ashamed of, but nothing to draw attention to either. We're normal, just like everyone else. Some things are, well, not exactly secret, more private, to keep within the family. Just in case. In case of what, I've never been sure.

I struggle to concentrate all morning, and I can tell Archie's distracted too. He starts working on entirely the wrong problems in maths – algebra instead of fractions – and takes ages to notice that he's doing a different thing to everyone else. My mind keeps wandering. I can't help thinking that this was all my idea – what if everyone laughs at us, or no one's interested and it's a disaster? But also I can't wait. As soon as the bell goes for lunch, Archie and I run out of the classroom and head outside.

We put out the tables in a spot we know most people will pass. They're piled with card and coloured markers. The sun's shining and there's no breeze, so we don't have to worry about things getting wet or blowing away.

The Pride group are there first, but once they start writing their signs and I take their photos, a crowd soon gathers around, asking what we're doing and what's going on.

"We're trying to get as many people as possible at Larkhall to show their support for LGBTQ rights – kids from every year, and teachers too," explains Kai to a group of Year Nine girls who've gathered around the table, curious. "You just have to write a message here." Kai holds up a piece of blank card. "No swearing though! Or you can use one of these." On the table are cards with the slogans we brainstormed and googled at Archie's house at the weekend, written out large and colourful: *Love = Love, Pride Not Prejudice, Here and Queer, Love Knows No Limits...*

"You don't have to have your face in the picture," says Josh to a nervous-looking girl on the other side of the table. "We can just show your hands holding the sign if you like." She nods, relieved.

"What are you going to do with the photos?" asks one of the girls.

"We're doing a display for the International Day Against Homophobia, Biphobia, Interphobia and Transphobia tomorrow." Kai takes a breath.

"That's IDAHOBIT for short. The photos will go up all over the school tomorrow, so that anyone who walks into the building will know straight away that it's an LGBTQ-friendly place to be," says Kai. "You can do it in a group if you want."

They check each other's hair, choose their signs and strike a pose.

"My uncle's married to a man," says the tallest of the girls to her friends after the photo's been taken.

"Never!"

"Yeah, I was their bridesmaid when I was little. Just wait till he knows we're doing this. He'd love it. Here, let me take a photo of us too, I'll send it to him."

I'm running from person to person, taking as many pictures as I can. It's frantic and I'm not sure I can keep up. At last, I hear a voice behind me.

"Becky, sorry I'm late, I wanted to get lunch first, but I've got my camera, what do I need to do?" It's Prakesh from photography club, and a couple of the others are with him too. They'd said they'd help, but I didn't know whether they really would. Relieved that it's not just me and my camera any more, I point them in the direction of a couple of grinning Year Elevens, who are holding a sign which says *Come Out for LGBT*.

JOSH

I'm actually enjoying it.

At first it was a bit awkward. Standing there as people walked by, wondering if anyone would stop. An idea that seemed good in Archie's living room didn't seem so good now, in front of the whole school. What if everyone just ignored us? Or worse, laughed at us.

And it would all be Becky's fault, and mine for encouraging her.

I felt sick. I wondered if anyone would notice if I just went to the loo and didn't come back. But Becky would, and I didn't fancy her getting mad at me again.

So I stayed. And people began to stop at our table and get involved. Then I was too busy to feel sick or awkward or anything any more.

260

Well, I *was* enjoying it, until I saw Jayden sauntering over. I hadn't noticed till now just how much he's starting to look like his big brother.

"This is stupid. Why would I want to have my photo taken?" he says, his voice rising above the babble and laughter. "I'm not gay, am I? Not like Josh, eh?"

"You don't have to be LGBTQ to take part," Carli says quickly, shooting me an anxious look. "That's not the point. It's about equality for everyone."

While she's speaking, I step forward. I should be the one putting Jayden right. She shouldn't have to do that for me. But when I open my mouth, no words come out. I want to be calm like Carli, but I don't feel calm. My fists are clenched in my pockets and my face is going red. I don't know what to say to Jayden, so I just glare at him.

He glares back. "Josh, what are you doing wasting your time with this sad bunch of losers?" he sneers. "Unless it's true, that you *are* gay too...just like everyone else in your family."

How does he know about Becky? Or is he just saying the first thing he can think of to wind me up? When I still don't say anything, he shakes his head. "Shame. No one wants a gay guy on their team, however good you are. My dad says—"

That's it.

"No one cares what rubbish your dad says, okay? Why don't you try thinking for yourself sometime?" I burst out.

A few kids still waiting to have their photos taken turn around to look at us. Carli puts her hand on my arm, I think to try and calm me down, but I ignore her.

Jayden leans over the table, knocking some of the pens off the side. "What are you saying about my dad?"

"Come on," I snap back. "I'm not saying anything. It's just that no one here cares what he thinks. Specially when it's something so stupid."

"You're jealous, that's what it is. But just cos *you've* not got a dad, it doesn't mean you can slag off mine…"

"Shut up. I don't *need* a dad. Not to tell me what to think. Or for anything. I'm proud of my family how it is, thanks." I take a deep breath and slow down. "Now, are you here for a photo or are you just wasting our time?"

Jayden doesn't say anything else. He's not used to people standing up to him. He turns, pushes past a couple of girls and stomps away. As I watch him go, I wonder, was I really that desperate for friends that I didn't notice what he was like? That I didn't mind?

I look back over to the table. Ms Bryant is standing there. Mr Ross is next to her, chatting to Archie. She looks serious. She must have heard everything. I wonder if she's going to tell me off, but instead she just gives me a quick nod and turns to Prakesh, who is hovering next to her with his camera.

"Okay," she says briskly. "I've got my sign, where do I stand? I've got a meeting in five minutes, so I need to be quick."

"Wow," Carli whispers to me. "What you said to Jayden, that was awesome. He was so out of line."

"Well…" I shrug. "It just kind of came out. It was all true though." And, as I say that, I realize that it was. Totally true. However much I might *want* to have a dad, or a brother, or to know the answers to all my questions, I don't *need* any of that to be okay or to be happy or to know who I am. I've got everything I need from Mum and Ima and Becky. I look round at the Pride group, busy taking photos or holding signs or just laughing and chatting. What's more, now I've got real friends too.

I'm so lost in these thoughts that it takes me a moment to realize that Carli's still talking. "You knew just the right thing to say," she continues. "Not like me. I got the group into trouble in the first place, didn't I? *And* messed up things with Becky. Perhaps I should keep my mouth shut a bit more…"

She falters for a moment, looking past me, through the fencing to the road outside. I turn to follow her gaze, but I can't spot whatever it is that's stopped her in her tracks. Eventually she drags her eyes away from the road back to me.

"None of that's *your* fault!" I tell her.

"You know, don't you? About Becky and me, why she's not really talking to me any more?" she asks quietly.

"Er…" I stutter, looking down. What's the right answer? What does she think I know? What am I supposed to know?

"It's okay," says Carli. "I *know* you and Becky talk about everything. You're so lucky to have someone in your family you can talk to like that. So, you'll understand what she's thinking. Josh, do you think it will be okay? I really *like* her, you know. Not like *that*, but like… well, it's just she was my first real friend here." She sighs. "I feel like I'm always making friends and then leaving them behind. Just waiting till the moment that we have to say goodbye. We've moved so many times with my dad's job that sometimes I think it's not even worth trying, it's not worth the hassle. But with Becky it was different – and now she's mad at me and I don't know what to do."

"She's not mad at you, honestly," I say, quickly looking over at Becky to check she's not listening. It's okay – she's busy setting up another photo with some sixth-formers and not paying any attention to us. "I think she's just embarrassed. I think she'd *want* to make up but, even though she talks all the time, she's just not very good at knowing what to say. I think she misses you."

"Mmm…" says Carli vaguely. Then suddenly she grabs my sleeve. "Let's go inside," she says. "Just for a minute, I, er, think we need some more pens. I can get them from my locker."

"But what about—"

"Don't worry," she interrupts. "No one will miss us. There are loads of people here to help now. Look, we'll be back in a moment anyway."

When we're inside the school building, instead of heading for the lockers, she turns down the corridor towards Ms Bryant's classroom. There's hardly anyone around. It's such a sunny day that most people are outside.

"Where—" I start saying, puzzled.

Carli puts her finger to her lips and glares at me. "Sssh!"

The classroom door is slightly open and there are voices coming from inside. They're muffled though and we have to strain to hear anything.

Ms Bryant's voice becomes clearer as she moves nearer the door. "Do take a seat, Mrs Peters," she says.

There's some shuffling and then someone else starts speaking, but they hardly say anything before Ms Bryant starts talking again.

"First of all, I'd like to say how happy we all are to have Carli at Larkhall and how glad I am that you've come in to catch up about how it's all going."

I gasp. Of course, it's Carli's mum in there. Carli must have known she was coming in today. What's she going to say?

"It's always difficult when a student starts mid-year," continues Ms Bryant. "But as her head of year, I'm pleased to tell you that Carli's done extremely well – making friends, catching up with her schoolwork despite the different curriculum, getting involved in activities. I've spoken with Mr Ross, her form tutor, and he says the same. I'm sure you must be very proud of her."

I look over at Carli. She smiles briefly and blushes at the words from Ms Bryant, but she still looks tense. She's waiting for her mum to speak.

"Well, thank you. I'm glad to hear it. It's the activities you mentioned that I wanted to talk about…"

"Oh yes," says Ms Bryant. "Carli's quite an athlete, I hear. She'll be a definite asset to our teams. I know some parents worry that training gets in the way of homework, but we believe it's really important for all students to have a rounded experience at school – not just the academic work. I'm sure you agree."

"Yes," says Carli's mum. "But I've not come in to talk about sports…"

"Oh?" says Ms Bryant blandly.

It's obvious that Ms Bryant knows exactly what Carli's mum is here to say, but she's going to make her spell it out. Ms Bryant's showing that she's in charge.

"No. Now, I don't like to complain, and I appreciate all that you've said about how well Carli is settling in, but to be frank, I'm very concerned about this so-called Pride group that I've heard takes place here. I don't think there's any place for that kind of…" She pauses. "… homosexual agenda in schools. Not at an age where young people can be so easily influenced."

I bite my lip to stop myself laughing out loud. It would really give us away if I did. But Carli's mum is talking nonsense – I mean, what is a "homosexual agenda" anyway?

I bet Ms Bryant will argue back. She'll tell Carli's mum that her complaints are rubbish or, even better, just give her a withering stare like when someone mucks about in science. She's got to. I wish we could see her face, but even following the conversation is hard enough.

Silence. When Ms Bryant speaks again, she sounds very serious.

"Thank you so much for raising your concerns, Mrs Peters. We always want to hear from parents, especially when we can clarify any miscommunication you might have heard. I'm a parent myself and I totally understand your worries. But I think I can reassure you."

"Well," says Carli's mum huffily, "I do hope so."

"You're right, we do have a Pride group here," says Ms Bryant very calmly. She sounds totally reasonable. "It's a new initiative, requested and run by the students and approved by the governors." She stresses the word "governors". "It's one of dozens of clubs we have – I mean, in a school of this size, I'm pleased that we have such a thriving extracurricular and pastoral programme. There's no compulsion for any students to get involved in any clubs if they don't want to, but of course, coming into Year Eight, they are now of an age where they can make their own decisions about how they spend their lunchtimes. However there is no *agenda*, Mrs Peters, of any kind, no agenda beyond encouraging all our students to treat each other with respect and understanding. After all, surely no one can object to respect and understanding, can they?"

"Well, no, but—"

She still sounds doubtful, but Ms Bryant cuts in quickly before she can say any more.

"Good, I'm glad we've cleared that up. Obviously, different parents will have different views on these kinds of issues, and the school can't – and wouldn't want to – stifle any discussion at home or encroach on the crucial role of parents."

"Yes," says Carli's mum vaguely. "Yes, the crucial role of parents, that's just my point…"

"However," says Ms Bryant, softly but firmly, "I must say we are rather, well, proud of our Pride group here at Larkhall. Over the last few days in particular, it's been clear there is *strong* support for the group from both students and staff, stronger than I had expected, and that's not going to change…" She stops. "Anyway, if there's nothing else…"

We hear the scraping of chairs being pushed back. Carli touches my arm and we tiptoe back from the classroom door and then run down the corridor.

I don't look at Carli until we're back outside. She's pale and her hands are shaking a little bit.

"What happened?" I ask her. "I don't get it. Was Ms Bryant agreeing with your mum? Or arguing with her? I thought Ms Bryant would stand up for the group more. You know, tell your mum how important it was and everything. But instead she just waffled on about respect and that stuff about the crucial role of parents."

Carli shakes her head slowly. "I don't know exactly, but, you know what? I think Ms Bryant did it." And her face breaks into a huge smile. "Come on, let's get back and do some more photos."

BECKY

By the end of lunch hour, I'm so tired that all I want to do is crash. I put my camera away and lean against the lockers for a moment to catch my breath. I don't even have time to catch up with Josh before lessons start again for the afternoon. I know something happened with him and Jayden earlier on, Archie told me, but then Josh disappeared at the end of lunchtime before I had the chance to see if he was okay.

I try to concentrate during the afternoon, I really do, but excitement keeps fluttering up inside me, making it hard to stay focused on French vocab. It doesn't help that I was so busy running around that I've barely had anything to eat all day. All the conversations I had at lunchtime are running through my head. So many people happy and positive, sharing their own stories.

We've got permission to go to the art block after school finishes to print out the pictures and work out how to display them all, ready for IDAHOBIT tomorrow. I can't wait to see them. Josh said this morning he couldn't make it after school because of football practice, but almost everyone else from the Pride group and from photography club are here, squashed into the art rooms: printing out pictures and info about IDAHOBIT, slicing coloured paper, gluing photos onto mounts. It's busy and noisy and people keep coming to ask me stuff about what they should do. Ms Bryant's there in the background, watching us work, occasionally answering questions, but mostly drinking her coffee and chatting with Mrs Mullen, who teaches art.

Archie comes up behind me, just as I'm explaining to a couple of Year Nines about where to leave the photos that they've just mounted, and he drapes his arm round my shoulder. He's beaming.

"Hey, Becks, look at all this. It's brilliant, isn't it?"

"Mmm, yes…"

I'm looking round to see if I can spot Carli. But she's not here either. She was really getting into it at lunchtime, but maybe now, despite everything we said, she's decided that she doesn't belong here after all.

"What are you thinking about?" asks Archie quietly.

"What? Oh, nothing." I shake my head. She's not here. I can't magic her out of nowhere, so there's no point in dreaming.

"Are you still upset about your mum?" he asks.

Of course I'd told Archie all about the scene with Ima after the party, as well as the real reason why Josh had disappeared on Saturday. He'd listened, open-mouthed.

"I'm sure she didn't mean it, all those things she said. I mean, she's not like that. It was just the surprise, I reckon."

"But I thought she'd understand, or at least that she'd believe me – even if she was surprised. Instead it was like she thought I was some kid showing off, just trying to be difficult. And then not saying *anything* good, just about all the bad things that *could* happen to me…"

"She does believe you," says Archie, squeezing my arm gently. "She's just worried, that's all."

"Well, she doesn't need to be. It's not like I haven't noticed how some people react to her or to Mum – or you. I'm not stupid. But so what? Most people aren't like that, are they?"

Archie nods. "I suppose not. I mean, just think about what we did today."

"Yeah, come on," I say. "Ms Bryant knows which boards we can use for the display. Let's get started putting up the first batch of pictures now."

It's hard to believe it's only a few days since Archie and I were working together like this putting up the decorations for Mum's party. Me directing, him reaching the places I'm too short to get to. We work quickly, in an easy rhythm, singing along to music from Archie's phone as we go, and soon the display boards are transformed into a blaze of colour.

But it doesn't only look good – when you stop and read the words and look at the faces, you realize what this really is. Not just a display or a photo project or a few nice pictures: it's a wall of love. I feel so proud of this, what we did together, that I can't stop smiling. It's so public, it's so in-your-face. It says we've got nothing to hide or be ashamed of. No one's going to stop us feeling proud.

Archie and I are so hungry that we buy chips on the way home. He texts his mum to say where he is and then we go back to mine, because it's nearer, to eat them in the warmth. I printed extra copies of some of the photos – the ones that Archie and I took of each other and the ones with the Pride group in – and shoved them in my bag. Now we spread them out on the table, careful not to get ketchup or chip grease on them.

Archie is just holding up one of the photos and saying, "I'm not sure about my hair in this one, see how flat it looks…" when I hear a key in the door, and Ima comes into the kitchen.

"Hi, Becky, Archie. You okay? I'm shattered," she sighs and, without waiting for an answer, sinks into a chair next to Archie. "I've been on my feet all day at work."

"Would you like a chip?" he offers, pushing the paper towards her.

Ima nods gratefully and takes a handful.

"Didn't you find the pasta bake I left in the oven?" she asks me. "I left a note."

"Oh," I say. "We didn't see it. We've only just got in."

"How was school then?" Ima asks us both, as she gets up to turn the oven on. "How come you're back late? It's not photography club today, is it? Or have I got the wrong day?"

"Er, well…" I say, suddenly feeling awkward about the photos spread out on the table. Ima and I haven't talked properly since the night of the party – not about me being gay anyway or about what she said. "We *did*

275

have photography club, an extra session."

"Oh?" says Ima, but she's not really listening. She's reaching down to pick up a photo that must have slipped to the floor. She looks at it, puzzled. It's Kai and Alex holding a sign which says *Love = Love* and pulling faces at each other. "What's this?"

Archie and I exchange looks. Then Archie says, "It's for our Pride group," at exactly the same time as I say, "It's for photography club."

Ima looks at us, waiting for us to explain properly.

"I mean it's for IDAHOBIT," I say.

She still looks confused, so I carry on. I just hope it's not going to start up the row we had after the party again. This might be just the sort of thing she was worried about. "We set up a stall at lunchtime…" I say.

"Not just us," chips in Archie. "Josh and Carli too. And loads of people from photography club and the Pride group."

"We had these signs and took people's photos with them. Teachers, students, everyone. Look…" I show her the photos, still without looking at her, so that she can see what I mean. Ima leans in closer.

"And people did this?" asks Ima slowly. "They didn't mind having their pictures taken?"

"No," says Archie. "We thought they might, but no one did – well, hardly anyone."

"Everyone *loved* it," I continue. "Honestly, they were, like, queuing up. We printed them out, and they're going up all over school for IDAHOBIT tomorrow. That's the International Day Against—"

"Yes, I know what it is," says Ima quietly.

"But also to show how the school welcomes everyone all year round," adds Archie.

I wait for Ima to say something. She's looking carefully at the photos, examining them one by one, touching them gently, but she doesn't say a word. I twist a strand of hair round and round my finger, watching her.

I hope this hasn't made things worse. I thought it was a good idea. I wanted to help keep the group going. But most of all, I see now, I wanted Ima and Mum to be proud of me, proud of our family. Just like I am.

She stops at the final one – Archie and me with our arms round each other's shoulders, holding up our *Queer and Here* sign and grinning into the camera.

She wipes her hand over her eyes and, when she finally speaks, I realize that she's been crying.

"Becky, these are beautiful. You all look so…happy. And so strong." She stops and swallows hard. "I'm sorry

I didn't see that before. It's just, I'm not as brave as you, Becky, or you, Archie. I took my fears and dumped them on you. That wasn't fair. I shouldn't have done that. When you came out to us, it was so brave. I should have wished you mazel tov, instead of making all that fuss."

"It's okay," I say. "Really it is." And all at once, I know that's true. It *is* okay. It is all going to be all right.

But there's still something bothering me. It takes a moment to work out what it is, but then I realize.

"Ima?" I say. "I know you've only just got in and everything, but is it okay if I go over to Carli's?"

"What, now?" She raises her eyebrows. "Can't you just call her if it's that urgent?"

"Well…" I say. Ima looks at me. "It's just…"

Her face softens, then she smiles. "All right then. I told you to treasure your friendships, didn't I? If you can wait a couple of minutes, I'll drive you over. I can drop Archie home on the way as well, if you like, Archie?"

"Oh, Ima, thanks, but it's okay, you don't have to," I say at exactly the same time as Archie says, "Yeah, a lift would be brilliant."

* * *

By the time Ima pulls up outside Carli's house, I'm not so sure this is a good idea.

I ring the doorbell, almost hoping that no one's home. Thank goodness it's Carli who answers the door, not her parents.

"Hi, Becky," she says, surprised but smiling. Just seeing her makes me smile too.

"Is this okay? Am I disturbing you?" I ask. When I'm nervous, like now, I get all breathless.

"No, it's fine. Actually I wanted to see you, there's something…well, I was going to call you, but now you're here. Wasn't it brilliant earlier? I couldn't believe it," she says.

"Me neither!"

"I bet the photos are going to look amazing."

"Archie and I put them up after school. We're only just back. They look so good, I had to come round. When your mum comes in to meet Ms Bryant, she'll see them all. Honestly, I think it's going to work. She'll see how much everyone in the school supports LGBTQ rights and the Pride group and—"

"Oh, Becks, that's what I wanted to tell you." She lowers her voice to a whisper. I lean in. "Mom came into school *today*. At lunchtime. She hasn't told me, but I know she did. When we were outside taking the photos, I saw her car."

Carli comes out to join me on the doorstep and pulls the door gently shut behind her, I guess so that no one in her house can hear what she's saying.

"Go on…" I urge her, although I'm not really sure whether I want to hear any more.

"Well, I followed Mom into school and tried to listen in to what she was saying to Ms Bryant. I didn't hear everything, but I heard enough. And, oh, Becky, it's okay, it's cool. I mean, it's not like Mom's changed her mind or anything, but I don't think she'll do anything to try and stop the group now. And even if she did try, Ms Bryant wouldn't let her. I know it. So, you see, I haven't ruined everything after all!"

I stand there silent on the doorstep.

"Becky? Isn't that great?"

"But…then, what was the point? We did the photos and everything for no reason?" I say, deflated. "We could have just not bothered, waited to do the assembly at the end of term like Ms Bryant said."

"The point was seeing how supportive everyone was – wasn't it awesome? Just think of all the people who didn't know about the group and now they do, and all the people who'll see the pictures and know the messages are for them…it'll matter to them. And it mattered to Ms Bryant too. I don't think she could have talked to my mom like that unless she knew how important the group was to us first. That's all because of you, Becks. Yeah, we all helped, but it was your idea."

"Well, maybe…" I can feel myself going red.

"Doing all this with you mattered to me too," she says, looking down at her feet. "It's freaky being in a new school, in a new country, trying to fit in. But you made me feel part of things, like I belonged. And that's why I feel so bad. Becks, I'm so sorry…"

"Sorry?" I'm confused now.

"I'm sorry about, you know, saying you shouldn't talk about your family in front of my mom. That was out of line. I don't want to be like that any more. I really like your moms and, well, I'm so proud that you're my friend. What does it matter what my mom thinks? Anyway, I've been thinking, perhaps she'll start to see things differently if she actually *meets* some LGBTQ people. Like, if she got to know you properly, she'd see you're not this bad influence or any of the things she's worried about. She'd just see what a good friend you are."

It's a lot to take in. I'd almost forgotten about what

Carli had said on the way to her house last week, what with everything else that happened that evening.

"I don't want to be your friend just so you can prove a point to your mum," I say. But I'm not angry. I hope Carli's right and that her mum *will* change her mind one day. But does she really mean it, I wonder, that she's proud to be my friend?

Carli looks up at me, then asks tentatively, "So we *are* friends again?"

"Friends," I say firmly, feeling one more thing fall into place. The cracks coming together.

All of a sudden, I remember what Neil said to Auntie Jackie, about how even if you think something's broken for ever, there's always a way to fix it – if you really want to.

After a moment, she says, "Look, do you want to come in properly? Mom's here and you can meet my dad. And I still haven't really heard how your mom's party was... and I'm sure it'll be fine for you to stay for dinner. If you want to."

"Well..." I say, hesitating. "I should go back really, Ima's waiting in the car. But...oh, okay, just let me go and tell her."

I run down the driveway to explain to Ima that I'm

staying and I'll text her later if I need a lift home.

When I turn back to Carli, she's grinning at me. I smile back, just as wide. She opens the door, and we go inside together.

JOSH

It's Friday night. And something's wrong. It takes me a few seconds to work it out, then I realize – I can't smell anything cooking.

I dump my bag by the door and walk through to the kitchen. It's empty. Just this morning's dirty bowls on the side. Nothing bubbling in the slow cooker. No casserole dish warming in the oven. We've been picking at leftovers from the party most of the week and I'm sick of them – each taste reminds me of that evening and that horrible day – but by now, even the last bits have all gone.

It's not just about feeling hungry though, everything seems wrong and out of place.

Something on the kitchen table catches my eye. It's

my tablet. I wonder why Ima's left it there – and then I see the note on top: *Thought you'd suffered enough.*

It's even charged up. My messages load. And there's what I'm looking for – one from Eli. Sent on Sunday. After I saw him, but still five whole days ago.

I want to read it, but at the same time I can't bring myself to look. I thought he'd never want to get in touch with me again.

But maybe this is just him telling me to leave him alone and never contact him again.

I push the chair back and walk over to the sink to pour myself a glass of water, putting off the moment when I read the message, but my hands are shaking, and I spill some on the table.

Just then, the kitchen door swings open, Becky bursts in and I knock the whole glass over. Luckily not all over my tablet.

"What are you up to *this* time?" she asks, looking at the puddle on the table. "You should see your face. You nearly jumped out of your skin. I thought you weren't supposed to be online – is that why you look so nervy? Cos you're worried about getting caught? If you are, then this is a pretty stupid place to try and hide – right in the middle of the kitchen."

"It was you charging around like an elephant that made me jump, all right? And anyway, look, I'm not hiding…" I show her the note from Ima. "Actually, Becks, would you do something for me?"

"Depends what it is."

"It sounds really stupid, but will you read this message for me? It's from Eli, the guy I met in Manchester. It's just, I don't know what he's going to say, and…"

"I know who Eli is. Of course you don't know what he's going to say until you read it, you idiot. Give it here." She beckons to me to hand over the tablet.

I slide it across the table to her, and then get a cloth to wipe up the water that's now dripping onto the floor.

Becky's reading for ages. Then she looks up at me. She doesn't say anything, which isn't like Becky at all.

"So?"

"He goes on a bit, this guy, doesn't he?"

"Come on, Becky. Give it back if you're not going to help." I reach over, but she hangs onto the tablet, holding it high above her head.

"Be patient! He says he's sorry about Saturday, he didn't mean to overreact. On and on about that. Er, what else? He says he's been talking to his mum about you and *she's* happy to talk to Mum and Ima if you want – he

286

didn't say their names, he just said 'your parents' – about how they can help you find info about donor siblings and everything. But only if you've talked to them first. And that he'll understand if you don't message back straight away."

I breathe out and, as I do, I realize I must have been holding my breath for a while. In a few days, from it being just me, I've got Becky *and* now I've got Eli – and his mum – on my side too. I've got a team.

"He doesn't say anything about being our brother though. Hey, he doesn't mention me at all! You did tell him you had a sister, didn't you? And about how great I am."

"Course I did." I correct myself. "The sister bit, anyway." I pause, thinking about how to say this. "I guess I don't know about the whole brother thing any more. I've been thinking about it over and over. He *could* be our brother, but who knows? Perhaps I *was* just kidding myself." It's so hard to say it out loud, but maybe I was. Maybe I wanted it to be true so much that I just made myself believe it. Maybe I was that stupid.

But Becky doesn't tell me I was stupid or laugh or anything like that. She just sits there and looks at me, not saying anything, but like she understands it all.

"But whether he is our brother or not," I go on, "we might have siblings somewhere in the world…and somewhere out there too, there's our dad, our donor, whatever you want to call him. He doesn't even know us, but he's still part of us. Amazing, isn't it?"

"Weird, you mean," says Becky firmly, then she smiles. "Well, I guess pretty amazing too, when you think about it. Maybe if we knew what he was like, it might just explain a few things – like your weird obsession with tidiness."

"Or some of your more disgusting habits!"

The front door bangs. Becky leans in, puts a hand on my arm and says in a special, slow voice, "Now, don't jump, but I think someone's coming in."

I swat her away. "Oh, shut up!"

Ima and Mum have their arms full and everything smells so good.

"You bought Chinese!" squeals Becky. She reaches into one of the bags and starts rummaging through with both hands. I know what she's looking for.

"You got spring rolls?" she asks.

"Of course," says Ima. "And crispy duck for you, Josh." She knows I can eat my way through dozens of crispy duck pancakes.

"Why've we got a takeaway?" asks Becky, unpacking the boxes. This is an unexpected treat.

"Well," says Mum, "my birthday was a bit…what shall I say? Surprising. It was a great party, and a lot to take in from you both afterwards, but what I'd expected was more like this – a takeaway with my family, and a chance to put my feet up in front of the TV. So this is my birthday, take two. Is everyone okay with that?"

"It may be a takeaway, but it's still Friday night, so I'm lighting the candles before we eat," says Ima. "Can you two put the food out properly?"

"Yeah," I agree. "Not just everyone diving in with their fingers, that's disgusting."

"I reckon we could all do with a reset, a chance to forgive and forget. It's Shabbat after all, time for a new start," continues Ima, as Mum lays out the plates.

"Is that why my tablet's back?" I ask and she nods in reply. "Thanks, Ima." She reaches out to give me a hug and I squeeze her right back. It seems like she's smaller than before and that I could pick her up if I wanted.

She whispers in my ear, "Never ever do something so stupid again. Okay?" And then carries on in a normal voice: "We've got something to show you both." She glances at Mum. "Maybe after dinner though? Better not get it sticky."

"There is another reason to celebrate," says Mum, once we've all sat down and are spooning the steaming food onto our plates. "Ima told me about what you've both been up to at school, as part of the Pride group. The photos and the messages. We're so proud of you, being prepared to speak out like that."

Ima nods. "I can't imagine anything like that happening when we were at school – can you, Anna? – or even if there was, being brave enough to take part in it like you two."

Mum shakes her head. "No way. When we were at school it was against the law, if you can believe it, to say anything about being gay, let alone anything positive. Teachers couldn't teach about it, and something like a Pride group, well…" She spreads out her hands, as if to say it was obvious that it would never happen.

"Oh, come on," says Becky, with her mouth full of noodles. "You're not *that* old."

"Afraid we are. At least, I am," says Mum cheerfully. "Don't forget, I'm fifty now!"

"Anyway," interrupts Ima, "what we're trying to say is that maybe we're not always so good at speaking out ourselves, but we think what you've done is fantastic."

Becky's already turning red, and when I say, "It was Becky really, the rest of us just did what she said – as always," she goes even redder.

Mum and Ima ask us, so we tell them more about the Pride group and the different plans we've got, and about Carli's mum ("I told you that's what she was like," says Ima with satisfaction). It's still awkward, but I even tell them a little bit about meeting Eli.

Eventually we all push back our plates. I feel so full that I can only just force down my final duck pancake.

"So here it is," says Ima, trading glances with Mum before taking an envelope out of her pocket. "I'm sorry we didn't show this to you two before. I guess that might have saved a whole lot of trouble."

She puts the envelope down on the table and pushes it towards Becky and me.

"It's the donor's profile. This is everything we knew when we chose. There's not much there, but it's yours if you want to read it. Nothing hidden any more."

I bite back my questions about how they managed to hide it so successfully in the first place, why it wasn't in the filing cabinet with the invoice. I'm not sure it would go down too well if they found out any more about how much snooping around I'd been doing.

"And there's another thing," says Mum. "I know there's a limit to what you can find out about the donor until you're eighteen, and I think that's right. I think it's best for us, for him *and*, most importantly, for you both. Hold on, Josh, I haven't finished… But there are still things we *can* do now – I'm sure you've already looked these up. We can join groups, meet other families – maybe even this Eli and his family. We can do that all together and we can do that safely. We'll support you, as long as you *both* want to do it, and as long as there's no more running off and no more keeping secrets."

"And we can talk about it more," says Ima. "If you want to."

Becky and I exchange glances. We both nod. I want to pause time somehow, or simply keep quiet and still so that this moment doesn't disappear. Saying something, anything, could break the spell. I think Becky feels the same.

"Okay then, now who's for ice cream? I'll go and get some bowls," says Mum.

Without waiting for us to answer, Mum and Ima disappear off to get the ice cream. Becky and I are left sitting at the table.

She looks at me, running her finger along the edge of the envelope. "You okay?"

"Yeah. It feels better like this. Everything out there. I was always rubbish at keeping secrets anyway. I hate it. But I'm sorry, you didn't get your happy-ever-after."

"What happy-ever-after?"

"You know, it didn't work out with you and Carli."

Becky shrugs. "Thanks. Really. It's gutting, but, you know, we're friends again, at least. Like you say, everything's out there now. No more secrets, right? And anyway, there's no point in looking for a happy-ever-after…"

"No?"

"No," she says firmly, grinning at me. "You know why? Because it's not the end, you idiot – it's nowhere near the end. There's loads more stuff that's going to happen to us. And it's going to be amazing. So, are we going to open this envelope or not? Come on, let's do it together."

She hands me the envelope and I open it. It rips a bit, but for once I don't care about doing it neatly. I hand it to Becky and she pulls out the sheet of paper inside, unfolds it and smooths it out on the table.

I take a deep breath. I know this piece of paper won't

tell us everything I want to know. It might tell us hardly anything at all. But it's a start, a new beginning, a chance to find out more about who I am, but to do it right this time.

Not by myself, not in secret, but with my family. Together. Becky smiles at me. Then we both lean over, heads touching, and start reading.

USBORNE QUICKLINKS

For links to websites where you can find out more about some of the issues explored in **PROUD OF ME**, go to usborne.com/Quicklinks and type in the title of this book.

At Usborne Quicklinks you can:

- Discover resources for donor-conceived young people.
- Find helpful advice and reliable information about being LGBTQ.
- Visit websites for more about being Jewish and LGBTQ.
- Learn about LGBTQ youth clubs and how LGBTQ/Pride groups are set up in schools.

Please follow the internet safety guidelines at Usborne Quicklinks. Children should be supervised online.

ACKNOWLEDGEMENTS

Josh and Becky's stories are made up, but they were inspired by the real-life experiences of LGBTQ families. Thank you to everyone who shared their stories with me, years before this book was written, as part of *Pride and Joy*, especially Bryony, Jackie, Jacob, Jess, Rajo, Shoshana and Victoria. Your experiences are much richer and more fascinating than anything I could make up!

I was quite a bit older than Becky and Josh when I came out, and – like their mums – am even old enough to have grown up under Section 28 (the now-repealed law which effectively prevented teaching about LGBTQ people in UK schools). I am full of admiration and gratitude for all those who campaigned, and still campaign, for LGBTQ equality, including my former

Stonewall colleagues, as well as for the teachers, school leadership teams, youth leaders and organizations who facilitate LGBTQ groups for young people – you are life-changers and life-savers.

There are so many more people to thank. Thank you to Yaël from Donor Conception Network for reading and commenting on this story and for your kind and helpful words. Thank you to Libby (who made sure Carli's voice was authentically and awesomely American). Thank you to Tamara and to Ruth (who both generously answered my questions about Liberal Judaism). Thank you to Sarah WH (for her behind-the-scenes knowledge of secondary school life). And, of course, an extra big thank you to Susie (my first reader, whose comments and insights proved invaluable again).

Thank you to my marvellous editor Stephanie, as well as to Kat, Jo and all the team at Usborne, to Sarah S for her meticulous copy-editing, Kath for the gorgeous cover design which perfectly captures Becky and Josh, and to Chloe, my agent, for finding this book such a good home.

And finally thank you to my family, Rachel, Esther, Miriam – and to my mum – for your love and support.

Also by SARAH HAGGER-HOLT

NOTHING EVER HAPPENS HERE

I wonder what people would think if they could see inside our house right now. If they could take the front off, like a doll's house, and see our little figures moving around inside. Dad loading the dishwasher in the kitchen, Jamie playing in the living room, Mum in her office and Megan and me in our bedrooms. Just like a normal family. All in the same house, but everyone separate. No one talking.
But everyone thinking about the same thing.
Will we ever be a normal family again?

Izzy's family is under the spotlight when her dad comes out as Danielle, a trans woman. Now shy Izzy must face her fears, find her voice, and stand up for what's right.

"A barrier-breaking, empathy-inducing story for all."
LoveReading4Kids

Read on to find out more...

"I know this feels a bit strange," says Dad, his voice shaking a little. "But there's something we need to talk about, as a family. It affects me the most, and your mum, but it will affect you too. I want you to be able to ask us any questions you need to, okay?" We nod, no less confused, but all listening now.

"Well," says Dad slowly. "Have you heard the word 'transgender' before?"

"Yeah – so what?" says Megan, looking up. My brain is whirring. This isn't what I expected. I don't have a clue what Dad is talking about or why.

"Being transgender or being trans," says Dad, "is a way of describing how someone might feel that they are born in a body that doesn't match their true gender. So, you might look like a man but you know you're a woman inside or people think you're a woman but really you know you are a man."

"Fascinating," says Megan sarcastically. "But what's this all got to do with us?"

Dad sighs. "*I'm* transgender," he says, trying and failing to keep his voice from wobbling even more. "What that means is, well, it means what I've known for a long time. That my body and who I am inside don't match up.

So I've been living as a man, in a man's body, but actually, I'm a woman." He turns to me as well and looks at us all seriously. "I'm going to start hormone treatment in a few months, and eventually surgery, so gradually my body will change to match who I am. But first I need to start living as a woman. Now."

He glances at Mum, and she nods encouragingly. Jamie's staring into space, I don't think he's really getting it. Megan's sitting dead still now, but I can feel waves of tension coming off her. And me? I feel like all the breath has been knocked right out of me.

One image fills my mind and I can't think of anything else: the bag, the shoes, the too-big clothes. They weren't Mum's after all – they were Dad's. It all makes sense. Except, right now, nothing makes any sense at all.

"It's nothing to be ashamed of, it's nothing dirty, it doesn't make me ill," continues Dad quickly. "But I know it's hard to get your head round, and that's why it's taken me so long to tell you. It's not going to change anything about how much I love you. But, well, I'm sorry."

He stops. It's like he's come to the end of the speech he's been practising. He's recited his lines, and now it's our cue. Except there's no script. There's no playwright to tell you what's happening next, or drama teacher to tell you how to deliver your next line. There's no band ready to play the next song. Just silence.

"Is it like Spider-Man?" says Jamie. "Like, there's Peter Parker and there's Spider-Man. And Peter Parker's really Spider-Man, but no one knows that he is. Like you're a woman, but you look like a man and no one knows about you either?"

"What the…" mutters Megan. "You're *not* a woman, are you? You're our dad. A man." Her voice rises. "How are you going to turn yourself into a woman? How can you 'know' that's what you are when you're not? Is this just some sick joke?"

Megan storms out of the living room, not waiting for any answers, and stomps up the stairs. She slams the door of her bedroom extra-hard. Mum and Dad exchange glances, before Mum gets up to follow her.

Dad turns to me. "Izzy?"

My heart is racing and my head is full of questions, but I don't know how to start asking any of them, so instead of saying anything I just shrug and try to smile. Dad puts his arm round me, and says, "You're a good girl, Izzy, I promise this is all going to be okay," and we sit there awkwardly for a bit.

Finally, he gets up. "I know it's a lot to take in. But if

you think of something later, you can always talk to us. How about I make us all a sandwich? Cheese spread, Jamie?"

Jamie nods eagerly. He gets irrationally excited about cheese spread. He'd have it on his Cornflakes if he could.

"Izzy, what about you?"

"Maybe later," I say. "Is it okay if I just go to my room now?"

"Perfectly pitched, this is a timely, gentle and honest story that will inspire conversations and encourage empathy." *BookTrust*

NOTHING EVER HAPPENS HERE

OUT NOW